The tool room door was open a crack. Surely Angel and I had shut it the day we'd been in there measuring and straightening.

I took another step and it seemed to me the crack widened some.

"Angel," I called, panic sparking along my nerves and surely showing in my voice.

She had a reaction that even at the time struck me as extraordinary.

Instead of saying "What?" or "Got a problem?" she broke into a dead run and moved so fast that she was in front of me in one split second after the tool room door had burst open. The man erupting from it was heading straight for us, and he had our ax in his hands.

━━━━━━━━━━━━━ ★ ━━━━━━━━━━━━━

Also available from Worldwide Mystery by
CHARLAINE HARRIS

THREE BEDROOMS, ONE CORPSE
A BONE TO PICK
REAL MURDER

CHARLAINE HARRIS

THE JULIUS HOUSE

WORLDWIDE.

TORONTO • NEW YORK • LONDON
AMSTERDAM • PARIS • SYDNEY • HAMBURG
STOCKHOLM • ATHENS • TOKYO • MILAN
MADRID • WARSAW • BUDAPEST • AUCKLAND

THE JULIUS HOUSE

A Worldwide Mystery/October 1996

This edition is reprinted by arrangement with Scribner,
an imprint of Simon & Schuster, Inc.

ISBN 0-373-26217-5

Printed in U.S.A.

My thanks to Reverend Gary Nowlin; attorney Mike Epley; Arkansas state park ranger Jim Gann; chemist Glenn McClelland, Dennis of the Georgia State Forensic Department; and Dr. Aung Than for their help with various parts of this book.
Mistakes are my own, not theirs.

ONE

THE JULIUS FAMILY vanished six years before I married Martin Bartell.

They disappeared so abruptly that some people in Lawrenceton phoned the *National Enquirer* to tell a reporter that the Juliuses had been abducted by aliens.

I had been home from college for several years and was working in the Lawrenceton Public Library when—whatever it was—happened to T.C., Hope, and Charity Julius. And I was as full of speculation as anyone else.

But as time went by with no trace of the Julius family, I forgot to wonder about them, except for an occasional frisson of creepiness when the name "Julius" came into a conversation.

Then Martin gave me their house as a wedding present.

To say I was surprised to get a house is an understatement: "stunned" is more accurate. We did want to buy a house, and we had been looking at fancier homes firmly anchored in the newer suburbs of Lawrenceton, an old southern town that itself is actually in the regrettable process of becoming a commuter suburb of Atlanta. Most of the houses we'd been considering were large, with several big rooms suitable for entertainment; too big for a couple with no children, in my opinion. But Martin had this streak that yearned for the outer signs of financial health. He drove a Mercedes, for example, and he wanted our house to be a house where a Mercedes would look at home.

We'd looked at the Julius house because I'd made a point of telling my friend and realtor Eileen Norris to put it on the list. I'd seen it when I was searching for a house for myself alone.

But Martin hadn't loved the Julius house instantly, as I had. In fact, I could tell he found my affection for the house strange. His arched dark eyebrows rose, the pale brown eyes regarded me questioningly.

"It's a little isolated," he said.

"Just a mile out of town. I can almost see my mother's house from here."

"It's smaller than the house on Cherry Lane."

"I could take care of it myself."

"You don't want a maid?"

"Why would I?" I don't have anything else to do, I added privately. (And that was not Martin's fault, but my own. I'd quit my job at the Lawrenceton library before I'd even met him, and as time went on, I regretted it more and more.)

"There's that apartment over the garage. Would you want to rent it out?"

"I guess so."

"And the garage being separate from the house..."

"There's a covered walkway."

Eileen tactfully poked around elsewhere while Martin and I conducted this little dialogue.

"You do wonder what happened to them," Eileen said later, as she locked the door behind her and dropped the labeled key into her purse.

And Martin looked at me with a sudden illumination in his eyes.

So THAT'S WHY, when we exchanged wedding gifts, I was stunned at his handing me the deed to the Julius house.

And he was equally bowled over by my gift. I'd been amazingly clever.

I'd given him real estate, too.

CHOOSING MARTIN'S PRESENT had been terrifying. The plain fact was we didn't know each other that well, and we were very different. What could I give him? Had he ever expressed a want?

I sat in my brown suede chair in the "family" room of the townhouse I'd lived in for years now and cast my thoughts around frantically trying to think of the perfect gift. I had no idea what his previous wife had given him, but I was determined this present would be more meaningful. Madeleine the cat spilled over from my lap to the cushion, her heavy warm mass moving slightly with her purring. Madeleine seemed to know when I began thinking she was more trouble than she was worth, and she would make some demonstration of an affection I was sure was false. Madeleine had been Jane Engle's cat, and my spinster friend Jane had died and left me a fortune, so I suppose Madeleine reminded me of good things—friendship and money.

Thinking of Jane led me to think of the fact that I'd wrapped up the sale of her house, so now I had even more money. I began thinking of real estate in general—and suddenly, I knew what Martin wanted.

Sophisticated corporation man Martin was from rural Ohio, oddly enough. The only obvious tie-in this had with his present life was that he now worked for Pan-Am Agra, manufacturing farming products in conjunction with some of the more agricultural Latin American countries, principally Guatemala and Brazil. Martin's father had died early in Martin's life, and his mother had remarried. Martin and his sister Barb had never gotten along with husband number two, Joseph Flocken, particularly after the death of Martin's mother. Martin had told me bitterly that the farm was falling to ruin because the stepfather was too consumed with arthritis to work it, yet he wouldn't sell, to spite Martin and his sister.

By golly, I'd buy the farm for him.

THE TRICKY PART had been thinking of a good reason to be absent from town for a few days. I'd finally told Martin I was going to visit my best friend Amina, now living in Houston and into the second trimester of her pregnancy. I phoned Amina and asked her if she and Hugh would mind letting their answering machine screen their calls for a few days. I'd call her every night and if Martin had called me, I could call him back from Ohio. Amina thought my idea was very romantic, and reminded me she'd be driving over to Lawrenceton soon, with her husband Hugh, for the festivities preceding the wedding and the wedding itself. "I can hardly wait to meet Martin," she said happily.

"Don't turn on your charm for him, now," I said cheerfully, and suddenly became aware I meant it. I felt quite savage when I thought about Martin being charmed by another woman.

"How charming can I be?" Amina shrieked. "I'm poking out to China, honey!"

I figured Amina probably had a slight convex curve to her tummy.

We closed with our usual chatter, but my jealous reaction gave me thinking material for that flight to Pittsburgh (the nearest airport), and on the drive west in the rental car to the town nearest Martin's family's farm. This town, Corinth, a little smaller than Lawrenceton, boasted a Holiday Inn where I'd reserved a room, not being sure what else I'd find.

You have to understand, for me this was an exotic adventure. Though I told myself repeatedly that other people traveled by themselves to unfamiliar places all the time, I was highly nervous. I'd studied the map repeatedly during the plane trip, I'd sat in the airport parking lot anxiously checking over the Ford Taurus I'd rented, I'd marveled over the fact that no one else in the world knew exactly where I was.

My first impression of Corinth, Ohio, was of how familiar it seemed. True, the land configuration was slightly different, and the people dressed a little differently, and maybe the prevailing architecture was more heavily red brick, more often two-story... but this was a small farming center grouped around a downtown with inadequate parking space, and there were plenty of John Deere tractors in the big sales lot right outside town.

I checked in to the Holiday Inn and called a realtor. There were only three listed; Corinth was modest about its salability. The company that advertised specializing in farms ("agricultural acreage") was Bishop Realty. I hesitated, my hand actually on the receiver. I was about to do some lying, and I wasn't used to it.

"Bishop Realty, Mrs. Mary Anne Bishop speaking," said a brisk voice.

"This is Aurora Teagarden," I said clearly, and waited for the snicker. It was more like a snort. "I want to look at some farms in the area, specifically ones that are not in the best shape. I want somewhere pretty isolated."

Mary Anne Bishop digested this in thoughtful silence.

"What size property did you want to see?" she asked finally.

"Not too big," I said vaguely, since I hadn't wriggled that information out of Martin.

"I could line some things up for you to see tomorrow morning," Mrs. Bishop said. She sounded rather ominous about it. "If you could tell me—are you actually planning to farm the land? If I knew what you intended to do with it, maybe I could select properties to show you . . . that would suit you better." She was trying awfully hard not to sound nosy.

I closed my eyes and drew a breath, glad she couldn't see me.

"I represent a small but growing religious community," I said. "We want a property that we can repair ourselves, and modify to suit our needs. We'll be doing some farming, but mostly we want the extra land for privacy."

"Well," Mrs. Bishop said, "you're not Moonies, are you? Or those Druvidians?"

Druids? Branch Davidians?

"Gosh, no," I said firmly. "We're Christian pacifists. We don't believe in drinking or smoking. We don't dress funny, or ask for donations on street corners, or preach in the stores, or anything!"

With an effort, Mrs. Bishop joined in my light laughter. The realtor gave me clear directions to her office, recommended a couple of restaurants for supper ("If you're allowed to do that"), and said that she'd see me in the morning.

I located the soft drink machine, bought a Coke, and watched the news while sipping a bourbon-and-Coke made from the second half of my airline bottle. I was glad Mrs. Bishop wasn't there to see the conduct of this purported member of a religious cult.

After a while, feeling strangely anonymous in this little town where no one knew me, I drove around, staring through the fading light at the town Martin had known so well growing up. I went past the ugly brick high school where he had played football. Through a light drizzle in the gray spring evening, I peered at the houses where Martin must have had friends, acquaintances, girls he'd dated, boys he'd gone drinking with. Some of them, perhaps most of them, were surely still here in this town . . . maybe men he'd gone to Vietnam with. Perhaps they mentioned it as seldom as he did.

I felt as if I were eavesdropping on Martin's life.

I had a book in my purse, as usual (tonight it was the paperback of Liza Cody's *Stalker*), and I read as I ate supper at the diner Mrs. Bishop had recommended. The menu was slightly alien—none of the southern diner standbys. But the chili was good, and it was with reluctance I left half of everything on my plate. Now that I was over thirty, gravity and calories seemed to be having a little more effect than they used to. When you're four feet, eleven inches, a few extra calories end up looking like a lot.

No one bothered me, and the waitress was pleasant, so I had a nice time. I took the light rain as a sign I should not walk or run tonight, though I'd virtuously brought my sweats and running shoes. As a palliative to my conscience, I did some stretches and calisthenics when I got back to my room. The exercise did relieve some of the cramped feeling the plane and the long car ride had caused. I checked in with

Amina, who told me Martin had indeed left a message on her machine not thirty minutes ago.

I smiled fatuously, since no one was there to see me, and called him. The minute I heard his voice, I missed him with a dreadful ache. I pictured his meticulously groomed thick white hair, the black arched brows and pale brown eyes, the heavily muscled arms and chest. He was at work, he'd told Amina's machine, so I could imagine him at his huge desk, covered with piles of paper that were nonetheless neatly stacked and separate. He would be wearing a spotless white shirt, but he would have taken his tie off when the last employee left. His suit jacket would be hanging on a padded hanger on a hook in his very own bathroom.

I loved him painfully.

I couldn't remember ever having told Martin lies before, and I kept having to remind myself of where I was supposed to be.

"Is Amina talking a lot about the baby?" he asked.

"Oh, yes. She's scheduled to take Lamaze in a couple of months, and Hugh's gung-ho about coaching her." I hesitated a moment. "Did you take Lamaze when Barrett was born?"

"I don't remember taking the course, but I was there when he was born, so I guess Cindy and I did," he said doubtfully.

Cindy. Wife number one, and mother of Martin's only child, Barrett, now trying to become a successful actor in Los Angeles.

Martin was saying, "Roe, is Amina being pregnant giving you any ideas?"

I couldn't tell how he felt from his voice. He'd spoken so much about Barrett lately I'd felt it wasn't a good time to talk about another child.

"How do you feel about that?" I asked.

"I don't know. I'm pretty old to be changing diapers. It's daunting to think of starting all over again."

"We can talk about it when I get home."

We talked about a few other things Martin wanted to do when I got home. By a pleasant coincidence, I wanted to do them, too.

AFTER I HUNG UP, I picked up the little Corinth phone book. Before I could reconsider, I flipped to the *B*'s.

Bartell, C. H., 1202 Archibald Street.

Now, this may sound fishy, but up until that moment I hadn't thought of Martin's former wife being in Corinth.

I discovered I was burning with the urge to see Cindy Bartell. A particularly ridiculous jealousy had flared in my heart; I wanted to *see* her.

Wise or not, I decided to lay eyes on Cindy Bartell while I was here. I took off my glasses and relaxed on the slablike motel bed, with an uneasy feeling that I was being seriously stupid, and wracked my brain to try to remember what Cindy did for a living. Surely Martin had mentioned it at some point or other? He was not one to discuss his past much though he seemed fascinated with the placidity of mine....

I almost fell asleep fully dressed, and when I forced myself to get up and wash my face and put on my nightgown, I had dredged up the fact that Cindy Bartell was, or had been, a florist.

The little telephone book informed me that there was a listing for a Cindy's Flowers.

I fell asleep as if I'd been sandbagged, still not having decided if my good taste and good sense would keep me away from Cindy's shop.

THE NEXT MORNING I showered briskly, put my mass of long, wavy hair up in a bun that I hoped would make me look religious, went light on the makeup, and cleaned my glasses carefully. I wore a suit, a khaki-colored one with a bronze silk blouse, and modest brown pumps. I wanted to look ultrarespectable, so Mrs. Bishop would be reassured, yet I wanted the religious cult front to be objectionable enough to tempt Joseph Flocken to sell the farm to spite his stepchildren. Unfortunately, I didn't know the location of the farm, since Flocken didn't have a phone listing. I was simply hoping I'd spot it driving around with the real estate agent.

I scanned myself in the motel mirror, thought I would pass whatever test Mrs. Bishop chose to give, and went off to have a little breakfast before I met her.

Her directions proved excellent, which boded well for her efficiency.

Bishop Realty was in an old house right off Main Street. As I entered the reception area, a door to the right opened, and a tall, husky blond woman emerged. She was wearing a cheap navy blue suit and a white blouse.

"The Lord be with you," I said promptly.

"Miss Teagarden?" she said cautiously, after a glance at my ring finger. Naturally, I'd left my huge engagement ring in a zippered pouch in my purse. It hardly fit my new image.

"I do have a few places to show you this morning," Mary Anne Bishop said, still obviously feeling her way with me. "I hope you like one of them. We look forward to having your group settle in our area. It is a church, I understand?" She waved me into her office and we sat down.

"We're a small pacifist religious group," I said with equal caution, wondering about tax exemptions and other hitches connected with claiming to be an actual church. "We like privacy, and we're not rich," I continued. "That's why we want a farm a fair way out of town, one that we can fix up."

"And you want at least—what—sixty acres?" asked Mrs. Bishop.

"Oh, at least. Or more. It would depend," I said vaguely. I had no idea how big the Bartell/Flocken farm was.

"Excuse me for asking, but I was wondering why your group was interested in this part of Ohio. You seem southern, and there is so much farming land available down there..."

"God told us to come here," I said.

"Oh," Mrs. Bishop said blankly. She shrugged her broad shoulders and assumed her Selling Smile. "Well, let's go find that place that's just right for you. We'll go in my Bronco, since we're looking at farms."

So for the whole morning I drove around in rural Ohio with Mary Anne Bishop, looking at fields and fences and run-down farmhouses, thinking about how cold and isolated some of these farms would be in winter, how the land would look covered with snow. It made me shiver to imagine it.

None of these farms was Martin's.

How on earth could I get her to show me the right place? Evidently Flocken hadn't listed it with anyone, was just sitting on it to keep Martin and Barby out. I began to hate Joseph Flocken, sight unseen.

We returned to town for lunch, after which Mary Anne excused herself to recheck the afternoon's appointments. I sat alone in the waiting room and fretted about seeing the right property. Even after that, maybe he wouldn't sell to me. I got up to look in the mirror on the wall above a tiny decorative table, a little closer to Mary Anne's office. My hair, which leads its own life, was escaping from the bun in a tightly waving chestnut nimbus. I began repair work.

If I listened really hard, I found, I could make out Mary Anne's words.

"So I'll bring her out this afternoon, Inez, if you're ready. No, she doesn't wear funny clothes or anything like that. She's tiny, and young, and she's wearing a suit that cost a mint..."

Damn! I should have gone and picked out something at WalMart.

"...but she's very polite and not at all weird. A real southern accent, you-all!"

I winced.

"No, I don't think the pastor would mind," Mary Anne said persuasively. "This group evidently doesn't drink, smoke, or believe in having guns. They can only have one wife. It sounds pretty respectable, and if they're off in the country by themselves...well, I know, but she has the money, it seems...okay, see you in a little while."

Mary Anne strode out of her office with a bright face and a sheaf of papers on the various places we'd see this afternoon. My heart sank down to join my spirits.

It was a long afternoon. I learned more about agriculture in mideastern Ohio than I ever wanted to know. I met many nice people who really wanted to sell their farms, and felt sorry for most of them, victims of our economic times. But I couldn't afford *all* those farms.

By four o'clock I'd toured everything Mary Anne Bishop had lined up. There were three more places to see the next morning. I was pretending to consider seriously two of the properties we'd looked at, but found sufficient fault with them to make her eager for tomorrow. We were pretty sick of each other by the time I got in my rental car, which had been parked at her office all day. I'd tried a couple of times to steer her conversation toward the years Martin had been growing up here, but she'd never mentioned the Bartells, though she and her husband were both natives of the town.

I missed Martin dreadfully.

I was almost through with my paperback, so when I saw a bookstore on my way back to the motel, I pulled into its parking lot with happy anticipation. Any place books are massed together makes me feel at home. It was a small, pleasant shop in a little strip with a dry cleaner's and a hair salon. A bell over the door tinkled as I went in, and a gray-haired woman on a stool behind the cash register looked up from her own paperback as I paused just inside the door, savoring the feeling of being surrounded by words.

"Do you want anything in particular?" she asked politely. Her glasses matched her hair, and she was wearing, unfortunately, fuchsia. But her smile was wonderful and her voice was rich.

"Just looking. Where are your mysteries?"

"Right wall toward the rear," she said, and went back to her book.

I had a happy fifteen or twenty minutes. I found a new James Lee Burke and an Adam Hall I hadn't read. The true crime section was disappointing, but I was willing to forgive that. Not everyone was a buff, like me.

The woman rang up my books with the same cheerful live-and-let-live air. Without thinking at all, I asked her where Cindy's Flowers might be.

"Around the corner and one block down," she said succinctly, and reopened her book.

I started my rental car and hesitated for maybe thirty seconds before going to Cindy's Flowers instead of the Holiday Inn.

IT LOOKED like a prosperous place on the outside, with a very pretty Easter-decorated front window. I powdered my nose and inexplicably took the pins out of my hair and brushed it out before I left the car. The front of the store held displays of both silk flowers and live plants, and some samples of special arrangements for weddings and funerals. There was a huge refrigerator case, a small counter for paying. The large work area in the back was almost totally open to view. Two women were working there. One, an artificial blond in her fifties, was putting white lilies on a styrofoam cross. The other, who had very short dark hair and was about ten years younger, seemed to be making a "congratulations on the male baby" bouquet in a blue straw basket shaped like a bassinet. Being a florist was a rites-of-passage occupation, like being a caterer—or a minister.

The women glanced at each other to see who was going to help me, and the dark-haired woman said, "You finish, Ruth, you're almost done." She came forward to help me silently and quickly in her practical Nikes, ready to listen but obviously in a hurry.

"What can I do for you?" she asked.

She had large dark eyes and a pixie haircut. Her face and her whole body were lean. She was beautifully made up and wore bifocals. Her nails were long and oval and covered with clear polish.

"Um. I'm just here for a couple of days, and I suddenly realized my mother's birthday is tomorrow. I'd like to send her some flowers."

"From the sunny South," she commented, as she picked up a pad and pen. "What did you have in mind?"

I wasn't used to being so identifiable. Every time I opened my mouth, people knew one thing about me for sure; I wasn't from around here.

"Mixed spring flowers, something around forty dollars," I said at random.

She wrote that down. "Where are you from?" she asked suddenly, without looking up.

"Georgia."

Her pen stopped for a second.

"Where do you want these sent?"

Uh-oh. I'd walked right into this. If I'd had the brains God gave a goat, I'd have sent the flowers to Amina, but since I'd said they were for my mother, I felt stupidly obliged to send them to my mother. I had sustained a deception all day, and perhaps I was just tired of deceiving.

"Twelve-fourteen Plantation Drive, Lawrenceton, Georgia."

She kept writing steadily, and I shed an inaudible sigh of relief.

"It's an hour later in Georgia, so I don't know if I can get anything there today," Cindy Bartell pointed out. "I'll call first thing in the morning, and I'll do my best to find someone who can deliver them tomorrow. Will that do?"

She looked up, her eyes questioning.

"That'll be fine," I said weakly.

"You have a local number?"

"The Holiday Inn." She was past being pretty; she was striking. She was a good six inches taller than I.

"How'd you want to pay?"

"What?"

"Cash? Credit card? Check?"

"Cash," I said firmly, because that way I wouldn't have to give her my name. I thought I was being crafty.

I'd been watching the blond woman work on the funeral cross; I always like to watch other people do something well. When I looked back at Cindy Bartell, I caught her staring at me. She glanced down at my left hand, but of course my engagement ring was still zippered in my purse. "Do you have relatives here, Miss?"

"No," I said with a bland smile. And I handed over my money.

I am not totally without resources.

As I PICKED UP supper from a fast food restaurant and took it to the Holiday Inn, I wondered why I'd done such a stupid thing. I couldn't come up with a very satisfactory answer. I hadn't given Martin's past life much thought, and I'd been overwhelmed with sudden curiosity. Surely prospective wife number two always wonders about wife number one?

I watched the news as I ate, my book propped up in front of me to occupy my eyes during the ads. It was a relief to be myself after pretending to be someone else all day. While I enjoyed imagining this or that in my head from time to time, sustained deception was another matter.

The knock at my door scared me out of my wits.

No one knew where I was except Amina, and she was in Houston.

I pitched the remains of my supper in the trash on my way to the door. I'd put the chain on. Now I opened the door a crack.

Cindy Bartell was standing there looking tense and miserable.

"Hi," I said tentatively.

"Can I come in?"

I had some bad thoughts: "Rejected Wife Murders Bride-to-Be in Motel Room."

She interpreted my hesitation correctly. "Whoever you are, I don't mean you any harm," she said earnestly, as embarrassed by the melodrama as I was.

I opened the door and stood aside.

"Are you..." She stood in the middle of the floor and twisted her keys around and around. "Are you Martin's new fiancée?"

"Yes," I said, after a moment's thought.

"Then I'm not making a fool of myself." She looked relieved.

I thought that remained to be seen. There was an awkward pause. Now we *really* didn't know what to say.

"As you know," she began, "or I think you know?" She paused to raise her eyebrows interrogatively. I nodded. "So you know I'm, was, Martin's wife."

"Yes."

"Martin doesn't know you're here."

"No. I'm here to buy his wedding present." I indicated she should have one of the two uncomfortable chairs on either side of the round table. She sat on the edge of it, doing the thing with the key ring again.

"He told Barrett he was getting married again, and Barrett called me," she explained. "Barrett said his dad told him you were very small," she added wryly, "and he wasn't kidding."

"For Martin's wedding present," I said steadily, "I want to buy him the farm he grew up on. Can you tell me where it is? I haven't told the realtor I want to see this one particular farm because of course she'll know I want it for some reason, and Joseph Flocken won't sell to me if he knows I'm going to give it to Martin."

"You're right, he won't. I'll tell you what you need to know. But then I'm going to give you some advice. You're a lot younger than me." She sighed.

"It's a good idea, getting the farm for him," she began. "He always hated someone else having it, someone else letting it fall into ruin. But Joseph always had it in for Martin, in particular, though he wasn't too fond of Barby. I'm not either, for that matter. One of the disadvantages of being married to Martin is that Barby becomes your sister-in-law...I'm sorry, I promised myself I wasn't going to be bitchy.

Barby had a hard time as a teenager. The reason the blood's so bad between the kids and Flocken—Martin'll never tell you this, Barby told me—she got pregnant when she was sixteen, and when Mr. Flocken found out, he stood up in front of the whole church—not a mainstream church, one of these little off-sects—or off sex, ha!—and told everyone in the church about it, with Barby sitting right there, and asked their advice—so she got sent to one of those homes and missed a year of school and had her baby, and gave it up for adoption. And nothing ever happened to the kid who was the *dad,* of *course,* he just went around town telling everyone what a slut she was, and what a stud he was. So Martin beat him up and blackened Mr. Flocken's eye.''

What a dreadful story. I tried to imagine being publicly denounced in that fashion, and cringed at the thought.

"Okay, the farm is south of town on Route 8, and you can't see the house from the road, but there's a mailbox with 'Flocken' on it by the gate.''

I copied the directions onto the little pad the motel left in the drawer below the telephone. "Thanks,'' I told her. And I braced myself for the advice.

"Martin has a lot of good qualities,'' she said unexpectedly.

She was giving the good news before the bad.

"But you don't know everything about him,'' she went on slowly.

I had long suspected that.

"I don't want to know unless he tells me,'' I said.

That stopped her dead. And I couldn't quite believe that had come out of my mouth. "Don't tell me," I said. "He has to."

"He never will," she said with calm certainty. Then her mouth twisted. "I'm not trying to be bitchy, and I wish you luck—I think. He never was bad to me. He just never told me everything."

I watched her while she stared into a corner of the room, gathering her strength around her, regretting already her display of emotion. Then she just got up and left.

It took everything I had not to get up and run after her.

THE NEXT MORNING I met Mary Anne Bishop at her office. I was in a brisk frame of mind. I asked her which farms we were to see today, looked at the spec sheets, and asked that we see the ones on Route 8 first. Looking a little puzzled, she agreed, and off we went. I looked carefully at each mailbox as we passed, and spotted one labeled "Flocken" just before the farm we'd come to see, which we toured quickly. I paved the way by telling Mary Anne that the area felt right, but the farmhouse was too small. On our way back to town, I asked her about the road that led from the mailbox over a low hill. Presumably, the farmhouse was not too far from that. "I liked not having the house visible from the road," I commented. "Who owns that property?"

"Oh, that's the Bartell farm," she said instantly. "The man who owns it now is called Jacob—no, Joseph—Flocken, and he's got a reputation for being cranky.'' But she pulled to the side of the road and tapped her teeth with a pencil thoughtfully.

''We could just drop in and see,'' Mary Anne said finally. ''I've heard he wants to move, so even though he hasn't listed the farm, we can check.''

The farmhouse was large and dilapidated. It had been white. Now the paint was peeling and the shutters were falling off. It was two-story, undistinguished, blocky. The barn to the right side and back a hundred yards or so was in much worse shape. It had housed no animals for some time, apparently. A rusted tractor sat lopsidedly in a field of weeds and mud.

A tall, spare man came out of the screeching screen door. He didn't have his teeth in, and he was leaning heavily on a cane. But he was shaven and his overalls were clean.

''Good morning, Mr. Flocken!'' Mary Anne said. ''This lady is in the market for a farm, and she wanted to know if she could take a look at yours.''

Joseph Flocken didn't speak for a long moment. He looked at me suspiciously.

I looked straight back at him, trying hard to keep my face guileless.

''I represent the Workers for the Lord,'' I said, making it up on the spot. ''We want to buy a farm in this area that needs work, a secluded farm that we can renovate. When the work is done, we'll use the dormitories we build as shelter for our members.''

"Why this farm?" he asked, speaking for the first time.

Mary Anne looked at me. Why indeed?

"Not only does it meet the criteria my church lays down for me," I said staunchly, praying for forgiveness, "but God guided me here."

Out of the corner of my eye, I could see Mary Anne looking over the mess of mud and weeds dubiously. Perhaps she was thinking God apparently had it in for me.

"Well, then, look around," Joseph Flocken said abruptly. "Then come on in and look at the house."

There wasn't much to look at outside, so we murmured together about acreage and rights-of-way and wells, and then went inside.

Martin's childhood home.

I gave Flocken some credit for trying to keep the kitchen, the downstairs bathroom, and his bedroom clean. Beyond that he had not troubled, and observing the pain it caused him to move, I could not blame him. I tried to imagine Martin as a child running out this kitchen door to play, climbing up the stairs to the second floor to go to bed, but I just could not do it. Despite the immeasurable difference loving parents would have made, I could not see this place as anything but lonely and bleak. So great was my wish to be away that I negotiated for the farm in an abstract way. Flocken obviously relished details of how the church members would have to work their butts off to build their own shelter, so I managed several references to the strict work habits my church required and encouraged. He nodded his gray head in agreement. This man did not want anyone to have a free ride, or even a pleasant one.

He and Mary Anne began to discuss the selling price, and suddenly I realized I had won. All it took was someone asking, someone he was convinced Barby and Martin would not want the farm to go to.

I wanted to *leave*.

I leaned forward and looked into his mean old eyes.

"I'll give you this much and no more," I said, and told him the sum.

Mary Anne said, "That's a fair price."

He said, "It's worth more."

"No, it's not," I snapped.

He looked taken aback. "You're a tough little thing," he said finally. "All right, then. I don't think I can take another winter here, and my sister in Cleveland has a spare bedroom she says I can have."

And just like that, it was accomplished.

I shook his hand with reluctance; but it had to be done.

TWO

THE PURCHASE went swiftly since there was no loan to approve. I'd thought I'd have to do a lot by mail, or perhaps make a return trip, but it wasn't necessary, to my relief. The essential work had been accomplished after three days were up. By the time I drove my rental car back to the airport in Pittsburgh, I'd paid two more visits to the bookshop, eaten in every restaurant in town, and rigorously avoided Cindy's Flowers. If I could have announced who I really was to someone, I might have passed the time with people who knew the man I loved, but I had to stay in character when I wasn't in my motel room. The chances seemed distant that someone would find out the real reason I wanted the farm, someone who liked Joseph Flocken enough to tell him. But I couldn't risk it. So I was virtuous, and ran in the morning, tried not to eat too much out of sheer boredom, cruised all the local shopping, and was heartily sick of Corinth, Ohio, by the time I left.

I swore I'd never wear my hair in a bun again.

I wanted Martin to meet me at the airport, so passionately I could taste it, but of course he'd want to know why he was meeting a flight from Pennsylvania, and I didn't want to give him his wedding present in the airport.

When I got off the plane in Atlanta I felt more relaxed than I had in a week. Carrying my luggage as though it were feather-light, I located my old car in the longer-term parking, paid the exorbitant amount it took to get it out, and drove off to Lawrenceton reveling in the familiarity of home, home, home.

When I passed the Pan-Am Agra plant on my way in to town, I had to stop.

I had only been in the plant a couple of times before, and felt very much out of place. At least Martin's secretary knew who I was.

"I'm glad you're back," Mrs. Sands said warmly, her grandmotherly voice at odds with the luridly dyed black hair and lavender suit. "Maybe now he'll be happier."

"Something wrong?"

"Oh, he got some mail from South America that made him angry, and he was on the phone all day that day, but he's back to normal now, just about. Go on in."

But I knocked, because he was at work; so he was looking up when I came in.

He dropped his pen, rolled back in his chair, and came around the desk in a second.

After a few minutes, I said, "We should either lock the door or postpone this until tonight."

Martin glanced at his watch. "I guess it'll have to be tonight," he said with an effort. "I should have an appointment sitting out in the reception area by now. Mrs. Sands is probably wondering what to do. However—I don't mind keeping him waiting..."

"No," I said, trying not to giggle. "I have to confess, it makes me feel a little self-conscious knowing Mrs. Sands is sitting out there. Tonight, then?"

"We'll go out to eat," he said. "I know you won't feel like cooking, and I won't get through here until seven, so I won't have time."

Martin's cooking is limited to grilling steaks, but he never minds doing it.

"See you then," I whispered, giving him one last kiss.

He tried to pull me back, but I wiggled away and grinned over my shoulder at him as I left the room.

"Bye, Mrs. Sands," I said in what I hoped was a collected voice. It probably would have been more effective if I hadn't suddenly realized my blouse wasn't tucked into my skirt any longer. I scooted across the room quickly, catching just a glimpse of the dark-complected man waiting to see Martin; a man with a heavy, piratical mustache, thick black hair, and rope-like arm muscles. He looked more like a nightclub bouncer than a job applicant.

I called my mother from the townhouse to tell her I was home, and learned what had happened in town in the few days I was gone.

"Thanks for the flowers, Aurora. I don't know what the occasion was, but they were lovely."

I started. I'd forgotten all about sending the flowers from Ohio. I mumbled something deprecating.

"Have you seen Martin yet?" Mother was asking. She sounded as if the question were loaded. I could see her at her desk at Select Realty, thin and elegant and self-possessed, remarkably like Lauren Bacall.

"Yes. I stopped by the plant. But he didn't have much time. We're going out tonight." If I'd had antennae, they would have been pointing in Mother's direction. Something was afoot. "How's John?" I asked.

"He's just fine," she said fondly. "He's been planting a garden."

"In the backyard?"

"Yes, something wrong with that?"

"No, no," I said hastily. If I'd ever doubted my mother adored her recently acquired second spouse, I knew differently now. I could not imagine in a million years my mother allowing someone to dig up her carefully groomed backyard to plant tomatoes.

I hung up shaking my head, decided to put off retrieving Madeleine from the vet until the next day, and carried my bag upstairs to unpack, happily, in my own bedroom.

I SCRUBBED MY out-of-state trip away in my own shower. I dried my hair. I took a nap. After I woke up, I went down to my basement to pop a load of clothes into the washer. The neighbor who'd been collecting my mail brought it over. I thanked her and she left. I stood by the kitchen counter leafing through the assorted junk. Suddenly, I let all the pleas from new resort areas and all the sweepstakes offers slip through my fingers to land in a heap on the beige formica.

Perhaps because I was tired, or shaken out of my usual routine...I don't know why. Suddenly I was asking myself, Why am I marrying Martin? There were gaps in his history. He was more than he seemed. There were moments when I found him a man of frightening capabilities. He could be tough and ruthless and hard.

But not with me.

I was getting maudlin, silly. I shrugged physically and mentally, shaking off the dramatic notions I'd entertained. I sounded like the heroine of one of those romance novels, the gals who think with their vaginas. I tried to imagine Martin and me posing for one of those covers, me with my bodice artfully slipping, him with his "poet shirt" strategically ripped. Then to complete the picture I added my favorite glasses in their bright red frames, and the half-glasses Martin wore when he read. I laughed. By the time I had put on makeup and chosen a dress, one Martin had bought me and made me promise to wear with no one but him, I felt better.

Actually, he'd said, "Never wear that unless you're with me, because you look so good I'd be afraid someone would try to lure you away."

Maybe *that* was the reason I was marrying Martin.

HE ARRIVED at seven on the dot. I had the deed tucked in my purse. I was determined we wouldn't give in to our hormones, but would actually make it to the restaurant, because I'd had this movie in my head of us swapping wedding presents in a restaurant, and I couldn't get rid of it. I think we were supposed to wait until the rehearsal dinner, but I knew I couldn't keep a secret from him until then, even a short three weeks.

We went to the Carriage House, because it was the fanciest place in Lawrenceton, and our reunion was a fancy occasion.

We ordered drinks, and then our food.

"It's early to do this, Roe," and Martin reached across the table to take my hand, "but I've got your gift, and I want to give it to you tonight."

"I have your gift, too," I said. We laughed a little. We were both nervous about this exchange. I supposed he'd gotten me a diamond bracelet, or a new car—something costly and wonderful—but I never expected a real *surprise.* He reached in his coat and pulled out a legal envelope.

He'd changed his will? Gee, how romantic. I disengaged my hand and took the envelope, trying to make my face blank so he wouldn't read disappointment. I slid a sheaf of stiff paper out, unfolded it, and began reading, trying to force comprehension. Suddenly it came.

I now owned the Julius house.

I felt tears in my eyes. I hated that; my nose turns red, my eyes get bloodshot, it messes up my eye makeup. But whether I wanted to or not, my eyes began to leak down my face.

"You know how much this means to me," I said very quietly. "Thank you, Martin." I picked up my huge cloth napkin and gently patted my face. Then I fished my own legal envelope out of my purse and shoved it across the table. He opened it with much the same apprehensive look I must have had. He scanned the first page and looked away, over the heads of the other diners, blinking.

"How'd you do it?" he asked finally.

I told him, and he laughed in a choky way when I talked about my representation of myself as a religious cultist. But he kept looking away, and I knew he would not look at me for fear of crying.

"Let's go," he said suddenly, and groping for his wallet, threw some money on the table.

We got out the door, adroitly dodging the young woman with the reservations book, who clearly wanted to ask us what was wrong. I put my arm around Martin's waist, and his arm snaked around me, and I went across the gravel parking lot pretty briskly for a short woman wearing heels. Of course Martin wouldn't forgo opening my door for me, though I had often reminded him I had functioning arms, and by the time he had gotten in his side, he was really breathless from trying to tamp the emotion back down inside. I turned around in the seat to face him and slid my arms around him. Sometimes I am very glad I am small. His arms went around me ferociously.

He was crying.

MY HUSBAND-TO-BE handed me the keys to our house the next morning.

"Go see it. Make some plans," he said, knowing that was exactly what I wanted to do. I was pleased to be going by myself, and he knew that, too.

I showered and pulled on blue jeans and a short-sleeved tee, slapped on some makeup, stuck in some earrings, tied my sneakers, and drove a mile north of town.

The Julius house lay across open fields from Lawrenceton, the fields usually planted in cotton. As I'd pointed out to Martin, you could see my mother's subdivision from the house—if you went to the very back of the yard, out of the screen of trees the original owner had planted around the whole property, which was about an acre.

A family named Zinsner had built the house originally, about sixty years ago. When the second Mrs. Zinsner had been widowed, she'd sold the house for a song to the Julius family. ("No realtor," my mother had sniffed.)

The Julius family had lived in the house for a few months six years ago. They had renovated it. T.C. Julius had added an apartment over the garage for Mrs. Julius's mother. They had enrolled their daughter in the local high school.

Then they had vanished.

No one had seen the Juliuses since the windy fall day when Mrs. Julius's mother had come over to the house to cook breakfast for the rest of the family, only to find them all gone.

The wind was blowing today, too, sweeping quietly across the newly planted fields, a spring wind with a bite to it. The trustee for the estate, a Mrs. Totino, Martin had told me, had had the yard mowed from time to time and kept the house in decent shape to discourage vandals and gossip. It had been rented out occasionally.

Today the yard was full of weeds, tall weeds, but this early in the spring, they were mostly tolerable ones like clover. The clover was blooming, yards and yards of it, bright green with bobbing white flowers. It looked cold and sweet, as though lying on it would be like lying on a chilly, fragrant bed.

The long driveway was in terrible shape, deeply rutted, the gravel almost all gone. Martin had already arranged to have more gravel hauled in.

The huge yard was full of trees and bushes, all tall and full. An enormous clump of forsythia by the road was bursting into yellow blooms. The house was brick, painted white. The front door and the door to the screened-in porch were green, as were the shutters on the downstairs windows and the awning on the second-floor triple window overlooking the front yard.

I went up the concrete steps to the screen door opening onto the front porch that extended the width of the house. The wrought-iron railing by the steps needed painting; I made a note on my little pad. I crossed the porch and turned my key in the front door for the first time.

I threw down my purse on the smelly carpet and wandered happily through the house, my pad and pencil at the ready. And I found a lot to note.

The carpet needed replacing; the walls needed new paint. Martin had told me to pick what I liked, as long as avocado green, gold, and raspberry pink weren't included. The fireplace in the front room should be flanked by bookshelves, I decided dreamily. The dining room that lay between the front room and the kitchen had a built-in hutch to hold our silver and placemats and tablecloths, the gifts that were already accumulating in my living and dining rooms at the townhouse.

There were plenty of cabinets in the kitchen, and the cream and golden-orange scheme was just right. I'd have to reline the shelves; I made another note. The Juliuses had begun renovating the downstairs bathroom, but I didn't like the wallpaper, and the tub needed replacing. I made another note. Would we want to use the downstairs bedroom, or turn it into a smaller, less formal family room? Perhaps an office—did Martin bring work home?

I went up the stairs to look at the size of the two upstairs bedrooms. The largest one looked out over the front of the house; it was the one with a row of three windows with an awning to keep out the after-

noon sun. I was drawn to them immediately. I looked
out over the ridge of the porch roof, which was separate; the porch must have been an afterthought. The
impression from the front yard was of looking at a
large piece of typing paper folded lengthwise—that
was the roof of the house—echoed by a smaller piece
of notepaper folded the same way lower down, the
porch roof. However, this roof didn't intrude on the
view, which swept across the fields to a series of distant hills. No other houses in sight. The fireplace
downstairs in the large front room was echoed in the
fireplace up here.

I loved it.

This would be our bedroom.

Closet space was a definite problem. The double
closet was just not adequate. I went across the landing to the little room with no apparent use. Perhaps it
had been a sewing room originally? Could we build an
extra closet in here? Yes, it was possible. There was a
blank wall that would make a larger closet than the
one we had in the bedroom. And there was room
enough for Martin's exercise equipment. The other
upstairs bedroom could be the guest bedroom.

Books—where would I put my books? I had so
many, with my library combined with Jane's...I took
time for fond thoughts of Jane, with her silver chig-
non and her little house, her Sears dresses and modest ways; rich Jane, who'd left me all that money. I
sent waves of affection and gratitude toward her,

wherever she was, and hoped she was in the heaven I believed in.

I went slowly down the stairs, looking below me as I went. The stairs ended about six feet inside the front door and divided the large front room from the wide hall that gave access to the bathroom and downstairs bedroom, and another way to get to the kitchen, rather than going through the dining room.

What a nice wide hall. Wouldn't it look great repapered and lined with bookshelves?

I laughed out loud. It seemed there could hardly be anything more entertaining than to have a house to redo and enough money to redo it.

This was the happiest morning of my life, spent all alone, in the Julius house.

THREE

I PICKED UP Madeleine from the vet's, where I'd boarded her while I was gone. The entire staff could hardly wait until she left; Madeleine hated everyone who worked there and let them know it. Growls issued from her carrier all the way to the townhouse, but I ignored her. I was riding on a happy wave and no fat marmalade cat could make me crash.

I met Martin for lunch at Beef 'N More, and once we'd said hello to half a dozen people, we were free to talk about the house. Really, Martin listened to me talk. I set my notepad by my plate and had to keep pushing up my glasses as I referred to it.

"You're happy," he said, dabbing his mouth with his napkin.

"More than I've ever been."

"I got you the right thing."

"Absolutely."

"Would you mind if I left you with the whole responsibility of seeing to the changes we need to make in the house?"

"Is this a nice way of saying, 'Since you're not working, could this be your job?'"

Martin looked disconcerted for a second. "I guess it is," he admitted. "I want our house to look nice, of course, and be comfortable for us; I mean, I care what it looks like! But I have some business trips coming up—"

I made a little sound of dismay. "Trips?"

"I'm sorry, honey. This was totally unexpected. I promise in three weeks I won't budge." Three weeks from now was the wedding. "But there are a lot of things I have to tie up before I take off for the wedding and our honeymoon."

To tell the truth, the prospect of having free rein on the house renovations was very attractive. I felt he was dangling that as recompense for the business trips, but okay. I bit.

"What have we got in the next three weeks that I need to be on hand for?" he said, getting his pocket calendar out.

I whipped out my own and went over the schedule; a supper party, a shower for me. "Then," I went on, "we have a barbecue in our honor at Amina's parents' lake house, a week from Saturday. It's informal. Amina and her husband will be driving in from Houston for that."

Amina would be my only attendant. The fit of her dress and the chance of her getting nauseated during the ceremony added yet another note of suspense to an already nerve-wracking rite.

"Southern weddings," my beloved said darkly.

"It would be a lot worse if we weren't so old and established," I told him. "If I were twenty-two instead of thirty-one and you were twenty-four instead of forty-five, we'd have at least double this schedule.''

Martin was aghast.

"I'm not joking," I assured him.

"And then, at the reception, you just have cake and punch," he said, shaking his head.

"I know it's hard to understand, but that's the way we do things in Lawrenceton," I said firmly. "I know when Barby got married she had a supper buffet and a band, but believe me, we're stretching it by having champagne."

He took my hand and once again I felt that oozy, melty feeling that was disgustingly like a forties song.

"I heard from Barby," he said, and I kept my face smiling happily with some effort. My future sister-in-law wasn't my favorite part of the wedding package.

"She's flying in two days before the wedding, and she accepted your mother's offer of her guest bedroom. I'll call your mother and thank her," Martin said, making a note. "And Barrett called."

Martin's son called Martin about once a month, to recount his ups and downs on the road to an acting career in California.

"Is Barrett still going to be your best man?"

"He can't make it."

I stiffened, dropping all pretense at smiling.

"He has a part in a movie filming then," Martin said expressionlessly. "He's waited a long time for this part; he has lines and is on screen for several scenes . . . the hero's best friend."

We looked at each other.

"I'm sorry," I said finally.

Martin looked over the heads of the other diners. I was glad we were in one of the little alcoves that make Beef 'N More at least a tolerable place to eat.

"There's something I want to talk to you about," he said after a moment. The subject of Barrett was clearly closed.

I shifted my face around to "Expectant."

"The garage apartment," he said.

I raised my eyebrows even higher.

"I have a friend who just came into town from Florida. He lost his job. He and his wife are very capable people. I wondered—if you didn't mind—if they could have the garage apartment."

"Of course," I said. I'd never met a friend of Martin's, an old friend. He had made a few connections locally, mostly at the Athletic Club, upper-management men like himself. "You knew him from—?"

"Vietnam," he said.

"So what's his name?"

"Shelby. Shelby Youngblood. I thought . . . with all the renovations . . . it might be nice to have someone else on the spot out at the house. Shelby will probably work out at Pan-Am Agra in shipping and receiving, but Angel, his wife, could be there when he's not."

"Okay," I said, feeling I'd missed something important.

"When I found out Barrett couldn't come," Martin said, almost as an afterthought, "I called your stepfather, and he's agreed to be my best man."

I smiled with genuine pleasure. In many ways, it was easier to marry an older man who was used to fending for himself. "That was a good idea," I said, knowing John must have been pleased to be asked.

We parted in the parking lot. He took off back to work, and I was going to my favorite paint/carpet/wallpaper store, Total House, to start the Julius place on its road to becoming our house. But halfway there, I pulled over to the curb and sat staring ahead, my window open for the cool fresh air.

Martin, in his "mysterious" mode, had put one over on me.

Who the hell was this Shelby Youngblood? What kind of woman was his wife? What sort of job in Florida had he lost, and how did he know where to find Martin? I drummed my fingers on the steering wheel, wondering.

Probably this was the *downside* of marrying an older man who was used to fending for himself. He also was not used to having to explain himself. And yet Martin deserved to keep his past life a secret, I thought confusedly; I was hardly telling *him* all... No! I had told him everything that might make a difference to our life together. I wasn't wanting to know the names of his sexual partners in the past years, which of course he should keep to himself. But I had a right, didn't I, a right to know—what? What was really frightening me?

But we hadn't known each other that long, I told myself. We had plenty of time for Martin to tell me whatever heavy and grim passages from his past he wanted me to know.

I was *going to marry Martin.* I started my car and pulled back into the modest stream of traffic that was Lawrenceton's lunch-hour rush.

Because really, trickled on a tiny cold relentless voice in the very back of my mind, really, if you asked him and he told you, you might learn something that would force you to cancel the wedding.

The prospect of being without him was so appalling, I just couldn't risk it.

At the second stoplight, I swept this all neatly under my mental carpet as prewedding jitters and took a right turn to Total House.

There I made a few salesmen very, very happy.

I MET MARTIN at the Episcopal church, St. James, that night for our fourth premarital counseling session with Father Aubrey Scott. The two men were standing out in the churchyard talking when I arrived—Martin shorter, more muscular than Aubrey, more intense. It felt odd walking over to them under their scrutiny; Aubrey had been my escort for several months and we had been rather fond (though never more than that) of each other. If they were asked to describe me, I suddenly thought, they would describe totally different people. I stowed that thought away to chew at later.

Martin had met me when I was dating Aubrey, and consequently always felt extra possessive when Aubrey was around, I'd noticed. Now, he slid his arm around me as I joined them, while keeping their desultory conversation going.

"—the Julius house?" Aubrey was saying in some surprise.

I looked up, way up, at his mildly handsome face with its carefully groomed dark mustache.

"Her wedding present," Martin said simply.

"Quite a gift," Aubrey said. "But, Roe, won't it bother you?"

"What?" I asked, deliberately obtuse.

"The missing family. I've been in Lawrenceton long enough to hear the story, several times. Though I'm sure it's gotten embroidered over the years. Can there really have been hot food still on the table when the mother came over from the garage apartment?"

"I don't know, I hadn't heard that particular twist," I said.

"And it won't make you nervous?" Aubrey persisted.

"It's a wonderful house," I said. "It makes me happy just to walk in the door."

"Emily would be too nervous to stay an hour."

Aubrey always had to drag Emily Kaye into the conversation. I figured the sexual dynamics went something like this: Aubrey and I had parted when

Martin and Emily appeared on our horizons. Emily had the child Aubrey wanted and couldn't have (he was sterile) and Martin had so much electricity for me I felt the air crackled when we were together. But Aubrey had dated me first, and perhaps a little resented my recovering from his gentle "good-bye" speech so thoroughly and quickly. So Emily Kaye, his all-but-in-name fiancée, was sure to be mentioned whenever I saw him.

It's stuff like that that made me so glad to be almost married. After so many years of dating and not-dating, I was heartily sick of all these little undercurrents and maneuverings. I was ready to be devastatingly straightforward. There is no telling what my reputation for eccentricity would have become if Martin hadn't chanced to want to see a house my mother, the real estate queen of Lawrenceton, was too busy to show him. She'd sent me in her stead and we had met for the first time on the front steps.

The phone rang in Aubrey's office, and he excused himself to answer it. I seized the opportunity to turn Martin's face toward mine and give him a very thorough kiss. That was certainly one of the biggest differences in my relationship with Martin; the sex was frequent, uninhibited, and absolutely wonderful. My sexual experience was not extensive, though I'd had what I thought was good sex before, but I had found a whole new dimension to the subject with Martin Bartell.

He said, "If it's the suit, I'll wear it every day."

"I was just thinking about the first time I saw you."

"Can we go back and stand on the steps of that house again?"

"No, Mother sold it last week."

"Well—" Martin bent to resume where he'd left off, but Aubrey came out of his office then. The churchyard was getting dark, and he called to us to come in. We went in hand and hand, and while we talked in his office, the darkness outside became complete.

"I HAD SUPPER tonight with Shelby Youngblood," Martin said. He was leaning against his car, I against mine, side by side in the church parking lot. The security lights overhead made his face colorless and cast deep shadows under his eyes.

Martin was going to spend the night at his apartment since he was leaving early in the morning to catch a plane to the Pan-Am Agra plant in Arkansas.

"I should meet him," I murmured.

"That's what I wanted to set up. Can he come out to the new house tomorrow morning? That's where you'll be?"

I nodded. "Martin, what's this man like?"

"Shelby? He's . . . trustworthy."

That wasn't exactly what I'd expected to hear. A strange capsule biography.

"I guess I wanted a little more than that," I said. "Does he drink, smoke, gamble? Where does he come from? What did he do before he came here?"

"He doesn't talk much about himself," Martin said after a pause. "I guess you'll have to find out what he's like from his actions."

I'd made Martin angry. Perhaps he felt I was questioning his judgment.

"You know what I call the way you look now?" I asked.

Martin raised his eyebrows in polite query. He really was angry.

"Your 'Intruder Alert' face."

He looked surprised, then irritated, and finally he began laughing.

"Am I that bad?" he asked. "I know I have a problem talking about some things. No one ever called me on it before."

I waited a little while.

"I don't talk about Vietnam easily, because it was dirty and scary," he said finally. "And there are some people I don't talk about, because they're connected with that time... I guess Shelby's one of them. He's from Tennessee, from Memphis. We were in the same platoon. We were good friends. After the war, we hung around together for a while. We kept in touch. Maybe once every three months I'd get a phone call or letter, for at least four years or so. Then I didn't hear from Shelby for a long, long time. I thought something must have happened to him."

Martin turned to look at the floodlit church, the lights shining full on his face for a minute, making him look—old.

"I got a letter from him about a year ago, and we resumed the connection. He had married Angel."

Martin stopped abruptly and I realized I had gotten all I was going to get.

It was a start.

I WAS AT the Julius house by seven the next morning. I looked at each room, slowly and carefully, revising my room-by-room list of the changes that needed to be made. At 8:15 the carpenters came, followed me around, took notes, and left. At 9:00 the paint, wallpaper, and carpet people came, measured, and left. At 9:45 the plumber showed up, trailing a miserable-looking assistant with a cigarette stuck in his mouth.

"Please don't smoke in here," I said as pleasantly as possible.

The lanky red-haired boy, who couldn't have been more than eighteen, threw me a sullen look and retreated to the front yard, where I was willing to bet he'd leave his cigarette butt in the grass. After years at the library, I could fairly accurately predict which teenagers were going to behave and which were going to be problems. This one was a problem. I looked at my plumber.

"I know, I know," John Henry said. "I don't think he'll last long. It's a pain riding in the truck with him. But his mama is my wife's best friend."

We sighed simultaneously.

John Henry and I discussed the bathrooms, worked out a schedule (as soon as possible), and then he crawled under the house to check out the plumbing. "I'm a little scared to explore too much here," he confessed with a broad grin. "Who knows but what they're all under the house?"

"Oh, the Juliuses." I smiled back. "Well, I bet the police checked that out pretty thoroughly at the time."

"Sure. Still, I bet you wonder if they'll show up here somewhere. It'd give me the creeps, Roe."

"It doesn't bother me," I said dismissively, and turned to the open front door to see a stranger standing there. He was looking back over his shoulder at the red-haired boy smoking on the lawn. When he turned to me, I recognized the dark man who'd been sitting in Martin's waiting room the day I'd returned from Ohio.

This was Shelby Youngblood. He looked at me in that moment, and we had a good rude stare at each other.

He was about five foot ten, swarthy-skinned, with muscles that were truly impressive, even to one used to Martin's muscular build. His hair was a dusty black, shaggy, only a few threads of gray, and his mustache was the kind that framed his mouth. His eyes were blue, and he wore old jeans and a faded T-shirt. His hands looked broad and hard.

"Miss Teagarden?" he asked, in a pleasant voice. "I'm Shelby Youngblood." I'd expected him to growl.

"I'm glad to meet a friend of Martin's," I said honestly. "Please call me Roe."

We shook hands. His were very hard, ridged and scarred.

"Come see the garage apartment," I suggested.

I got my keys and led the way, out the kitchen, under the roofed walkway, over to the garage with the covered stairs running up the side closest to the house. I unlocked the door at the top, and we went in. Since the garage was not only more than wide enough for two cars, but had a deep storage room running all its width along the back, the apartment was larger than one expected from outside. It was a very good size for one person—it was basically one large open room. I hoped two people would be comfortable there. The bathroom was small but adequate, and more modern than the ones in the house, since it was the Juliuses who had turned what had been a glorified hayloft into an apartment for Mrs. Julius's mother. The tiny kitchen was not meant for producing a full Thanksgiving feast, but would be bearable for someone who was not an enthusiastic cook.

I looked at Shelby Youngblood inquiringly.

"Is this okay?" I asked, when he didn't say anything.

"It's fine," he said with some surprise, as if he hadn't realized I was waiting for his verdict.

"This carpet is mildewed, I think the carpet pad is, too," I said, wrinkling my nose. I hadn't noticed this the other time I'd looked at the apartment. "I'll replace it. Is there any color you particularly like? Anything that might match your furniture...?"

"Right now, we don't have any," he said calmly.

He seemed amused.

All right! What was so damned funny about not having furniture, about my wanting to know if their furniture was any color I should be mindful of when I ordered carpet! Didn't most people in their forties have furniture? It wasn't as if I'd asked about his racial origin or asked him to describe a shrimp fork. I could feel myself turning red.

"Angel and I haven't been in one place long enough to accumulate much," he said, and I nodded curtly.

"Then I'll rent it furnished," I said, and turned and walked out.

I stomped down the stairs breathing heavily.

I spied John Henry's wife's best friend's son going into my house with a cigarette in his mouth.

"Excuse me!" I called.

He stopped and turned.

This kid had an attitude, no doubt about it. He looked at me as if I'd crawled out from under a rock to question his God-given right to smoke in my house.

"Please put out the cigarette before you go in," I said as evenly as I could imagine, coming to a stop in the front yard a few feet away from the boy as he stood on my front steps.

He rolled his eyes and sneered. It was one of those teenage grimaces that make you amazed that so many of them survive to adulthood. Of course teenagers had acted like this in the library, and I had handled it then, but a few months away had desensitized me.

Already angry, I was now inwardly berserk. What this translated to on the outside was that I had my hands clenched in fists by my side, my jaw felt soldered together, and all I needed to complete my Shirley Temple imitation was to stick my lip out.

The boy dropped the cigarette on my wooden porch and ground it out with his foot. He took another step inside.

"Pick it up," suggested a quiet voice from behind me.

"Huh?" The boy's mouth was open in amazement at this novel idea.

"Pick it up and put it in your pocket," the quiet voice said, as if it were implanting a posthypnotic suggestion.

With a fearful stare over my shoulder, the boy reached down, picked up his cigarette butt, dropped it in his pocket, and scuttled into the house.

"Now," I said, pivoting on my heel, "I could have handled that by myself."

"I made you mad in the first place," Shelby said.

I tried to think that out, but couldn't while he was standing there looking at me.

"We should start again," he said.

"Yes."

"Hi, I'm Shelby Youngblood, a friend of Martin's."

"Hi. I'm Roe Teagarden, Martin's fiancée."

We didn't shake hands again, but regarded each other warily.

"I hope you don't mind Martin suggesting we live here," Shelby said.

That wasn't easy for him. He wasn't used to being beholden to anyone.

I blew out a long breath silently, gradually cooling down. I decided on simple positive sentences. "I am very glad for you to be in the apartment. I know that you plan to help out while the renovation is going on. I'm anxious to get it done as soon as possible. We'll get married in three weeks, and be back from our honeymoon two weeks after that, so I hope to have most of it done by then."

"If I start work at Pan-Am Agra before then, Angel will be more than able to supervise whatever work is left to be done," Shelby said. "And by the way, she likes light orange—I think she calls it peach—and green."

I could feel the tension ease out of my face.

"Will you go back to—Florida, right?—to get her, or..."

"Yeah. I'll fly back tomorrow, and we'll wrap things up there and start driving up here in maybe three or four days."

"Okay. That'll work out great." By the time the Youngbloods were in place, I should be more and more wrapped up in wedding plans, and it really would be a help to have them actually on the spot.

For the first time I saw how Shelby Youngblood had gotten out to the house. He was driving Martin's car.

"He really does trust you," I said.

"Yeah."

We gave each other another long look.

"Catch you later," Shelby said casually, and strode off, starting up Martin's car and driving off in it.

It felt very strange to see someone else in Martin's car.

I RAN INTO TOWN to tell the carpet and paint people they had a new job, and one that took priority. By great good fortune, they had a peach-colored carpet in stock. Since the white walls in the apartment were still in very good shape, I asked the painter to do the baseboards and door and window frames in green. I was lucky enough to find white curtains with a little peach-colored figure at WalMart (I was in too much of a hurry to have some made), and as for furniture...gee, this was getting expensive. I looked in the for-sale ads of the *Lawrenceton Sentinel* and called some of the numbers listed. By late afternoon, I'd found a very nice used bedroom suite and a couch and two armchairs in a neutral beige, and had run back to WalMart and bought queen-sized sheets and a bed-spread (green). The living-room set was in good shape but needed cleaning. I made a note to buy a spray cleaner, and then rushed back to the townhouse to get ready for the wedding shower.

As I sank into the warm water of the bathtub, I re-alized that I hadn't eaten lunch and didn't have time to eat supper. I was astonished. Meals were not some-thing I skipped without noticing. Well, I certainly hadn't missed the calories, but I wouldn't be able to keep up this pace unless I took better care of myself. I consciously relaxed everything from my toes on up, practicing slow regular breathing. I was going to enjoy tonight. I'd waited all these years for a bridal shower in my honor; by golly, this was my night.

Luckily, I'd decided in advance what to wear. I pulled the purple with white polka dots from the closet, put in the amethyst earrings Martin had bought me, slid my feet into one of my few pairs of high heels. After surveying my reflection, I added a small gold bracelet. I brushed my hair carefully and then put on a braided headband to keep the mass out of my face (and my drink, and my food).

Food. I hoped Eileen and Sally had a tableful. Maybe those sausage and biscuit balls?

My mouth watered while I swapped purses, and when my mother rang the doorbell, I was feeling ravenous.

My mother, Aida Brattle Teagarden Queensland, looked aristocratic and slim and cool as ever in a gorgeous royal-blue suit. She is a woman dauntingly difficult to criticize. Her clothes and behavior are always appropriate for the occasion. She always thinks before she speaks. Her extensive and successful business dealings are always ethically aboveboard, and her employees have excellent health benefits and a profit-sharing program.

But she is definitely not a woman you would run up and hug without a fair warning and a good reason, and she is not sentimental, and she never forgets anyone who does not deal fairly with her.

Mother gave me a careful, cheerful kiss on the cheek. She was finally marrying me off, enjoying all the mother-of-the-bride things that she'd been denied. And she knew I was happy. And she approved of Martin, though I sensed reservations. Martin was closer to her age than to mine, and that worried her a bit. (She had asked me if I'd seen his company's insurance policy, for example.) And, being my mother and extremely property oriented, she wanted to know how much money Martin had in the bank, what his salary was, how much of that he saved, and what his pension program was. Since it was impossible for her to ask Martin these things point-blank, it had been amusing to hear her try to maneuver the conversation delicately around to what she wanted to know.

"I'm willing to give her a full, typed financial statement," Martin had told me after we'd eaten supper with Mother and John one night.

"That would be too direct," I told him. "I don't know why she's in such a lather, anyway." (Though actually, my mother in a lather was pretty unimaginable.) "I have plenty of money of my own, safely invested, well protected."

"She's just watching out for you," Martin said fondly.

I had dark thoughts about why everyone seemed to feel I needed "watching out for," but considering my mother had a right to if anyone did, I kept quiet.

Now as Mother swept me into her superior car (she'd picked me up because she considered my old Chevette to be too plebeian for The Bride) she checked me over as though I were going on my first date, gave a quick little nod of approval, and asked me if I'd heard from my father lately.

"Not since he called me after he talked to Betty Jo about coming," I answered. Betty Jo was my father's second wife, down to earth, plain, and homey as all get out. When he'd fled my mother, Father had certainly run in the opposite direction. He and Betty Jo lived in California now, with their child, my brother Phillip, age nine. I hadn't seen my father or Phillip or Betty Jo in nearly three years.

"He said they were?"

"If he could take his vacation time then. He was going to ask."

"And you haven't heard back," my mother murmured, almost to herself.

I didn't say anything.

"I'll call him tomorrow," she said decisively. "He has to let us know."

"I'd like Phillip to be ring-bearer if they're coming," I said suddenly.

It was lucky we were in Mother's big Lincoln, because it was full of thoughts unsaid. Phillip had had a traumatic experience the last time he spent the weekend with me. They'd moved to California in a (to me) mistaken attempt to help Phillip recover, and he'd been seeing a counselor for a year afterward. According to my father's rare letters, Phillip was fine now.

Then, as we parked at Eileen's house, I caught a glimpse through the picture window of a table covered in white with white and silver wedding bells hanging from the light fixture, and Eileen carrying in a big tray of something sure to be edible, and Sally Allison, her cohostess, stirring a huge silver bowl of punch. On a table nearby presents wrapped in white and silver and pastels were heaped. Sally and Eileen were dressed to the teeth.

As I slip out of the car it hit me smack in the psyche.

This was for *me*.

I was getting *married*.

I put one hand out to the roof of the car and the other touched my chest as if I were pledging my allegiance.

I knew a moment of delight, followed by a groundswell of panic.

"Just hit you, huh?" Mother asked.

I nodded, unable to say a word.

We stood in the dark, looking through that window, for a couple of minutes. It was oddly companionable.

"Which way is it going to be?" Mother finally asked.

It was the first time she'd spoken to me as if I were absolutely grown up.

"Let's go in," I said, and started up the sidewalk to the front door.

FOUR

MOTHER AND I stood nervously in the foyer waiting to say hello to the first arrivals before being put wherever we were supposed to sit during the present opening. Though Mother was nervous, she looked as composed and cool as she always did, as though she couldn't sweat. But one eyelid twitched from time to time.

One of Mother's friends came in first, and then Amina's mom, Miss Joe Nell, one of my favorite people. And then the guests came too fast for me to talk much to each one; it was like a "This Is Your Life" theme party. The pile of presents rose higher and higher, and the room got fuller and fuller, and older women who had been my mother's friends for years mixed with women my own age whom I'd known all my life—Susu Hunter, Lizanne Buckley Sewell, Linda Erhardt, and several other—and women who had to be asked because of some connection to my life, like Patty Cloud, my mother's office manager, and Melinda, wife of my mother's husband's son, and a couple of women I'd asked just to say "Ha!" such as Lynn Liggett Smith (wife of my former flame Arthur Smith) and Emily Kaye (love of my former flame the Reverend Aubrey Scott).

After the usual twenty minutes or so of chatter, during which I answered the same questions six or seven times, Sally made a little speech about my upcoming marriage, including a joke about how long we'd all waited for that day—thanks, Sally—and then the present opening began. I had registered my color preferences in towels and bathroom items with the local stores, and of course I got lots of those, and toothbrush holders and wastebaskets and even a monogrammed towel rack, which left me practically speechless. I could hardly wait to show it to Martin, and picturing his face started a fit of giggles I had trouble suppressing. I passed each present around the circle of women so it could be admired and its giver complimented on her choice.

It was the lingerie, of course, that provoked the most oohs and ahhs. I got a leopard print teddy from Susu, which engendered quite a few risqué comments, and some silk pajamas from my mother in a champagne color, and from the shower hostesses a truly gorgeous negligee set in black lace. Showing that to Martin was going to be fun, too.

Sally and Eileen had popped in and out during the present opening, vanishing to the kitchen after commenting on a gift or two, and now they both appeared and took their place at the loaded dining-room table, Sally pouring punch into delicate glass cups and Eileen cutting and serving the cake on her best china at the opposite end. As the honoree, I was expected to go first, one of the other nice things about being a bride. We all made the ritual comments about how good everything looked, and about how we'd just eaten supper so we weren't sure we could jam in another bite, and then we loaded down our plates and stuffed ourselves.

Of course it was all good, but it could have been sawdust and I would still have enjoyed it. Some women reminisced about their showers and weddings, some asked Sally and Eileen for recipes, others talked about ordinary Lawrenceton happenings, others asked me about the wedding plans, and a few of the older ladies quizzed me about Martin and who "his people" were.

As some of the guests were returning their empty plates to the sideboard, a very old lady came to sit in the chair beside me that my mother had temporarily vacated. She had wrinkles like cobwebs gridding her face, her eyes were the color of bleached denim, and her thinning hair was snowy. She was wearing one of those flowered dresses that were the staple of Lawrenceton fashion. This particular example was sky blue with pink flowers, and the lady who wore it was the same thickness all the way up and down. This was Mrs. Lyndower Dawson, christened Eunice, but since childhood called Neecy.

"How are you, Miss Neecy?" I asked.

"I get 'long pretty good, Aurora. As long as the Lord lets me, I want to get around on my own," Neecy told me solemnly.

In Lawrenceton, we were a little worried about the Lord letting Miss Neecy get around, since she was still driving and tended to take the middle of the road and ignore little things like stop signs.

"Now, tell me something, Aurora," Neecy said slowly, and I realized we were getting to the crux, here. "I hear that that young man of yours has bought you the so-called Julius house."

"That's right," I said agreeably, tickled at Martin being my "young man" and curious about what she was going to tell me.

"They call it the Julius house, but of course it isn't really."

"Oh?"

"Of course not; those people just lived there a few months. It's really the Zinsner house, they originally built it and lived in it for oh, sixty or sixty-five years before Sarah May sold it to those Juliuses."

"Is that right?" Actually, I'd known that, but I didn't want to dam Miss Neecy in midflow.

"Oh, yes, honey, the Zinsners were an old Lawrenceton family. They got here before my family, even. And the branch that built that house was the last of the family. They built out there when town was two and a half miles away on a poor dirt road, rather than a mile away on a paved one."

I nodded encouragingly.

"I remember when they were building that house, John L. and Sarah May were fighting like cats and dogs about how to do it. John L. wanted things one way, Sarah May wanted 'em another. Sarah May wanted a gazebo in the backyard, and John L. told her she'd have to build one with her own hands if she wanted it. Sarah May was one smart woman, but that she couldn't do. But she had her own way about the porch. After the house was all but finished, she told John L. she had to have a front porch, a big one. Now John L. had already had the roof completed, and he didn't want to tear it up again, so that's why the roof of the porch is separate. John L. just put in guttering between the two parts. Then Sarah wanted a two-car garage instead of a one-car, and though they only had one car, John L. added another stall for another car. And then she wanted an extra closet, but John L. and her had a fight and he boarded it up to spite her!'' Neecy shook her head as she remembered the battling Zinsners.

"They're both gone now?" I asked gently.

"Gosh, no, someone as mean as Sarah May takes a long time to kill," Neecy said cheerfully. "She's over in Peachtree Leisure Apartments, a nice name for that old folks' home on Pike Street, where the old fire station used to be. I go to visit my friends out there from time to time, and I see Sarah May right often, though some days she doesn't know me. And that woman is out there, too, come to think of it."

"What woman do you mean, Miss Neecy?"

"That Julius woman's mother. Got an Italian name. Totino. Melba Totino."

I hadn't known the family who'd built the house still had living members, and I hadn't known The Mother-in-law (as she was invariably referred to in local legend) was still living, much less still living in Lawrenceton.

"There, you didn't know all that, did you?" said Neecy in a pleased way. "Not too many of us around to remember things the way they were."

"Thanks for telling me," I said sincerely.

"Oh, we old people aren't much good for anything except remembering," Neecy said with a deprecatory wave of her hand.

Of course, I protested as I was supposed to, and she ended up happy, which she was supposed to. I thanked her profusely for her gift of scented "guest" soap shaped like seashells, and that pleased her, too.

She got up to go and thought of one more thing to say. "That man you're marrying, Aurora, is it true he's from Chicago, Illinois?"

"Well, he moved here from Chicago. Actually, he grew up in Ohio."

Neecy Dawson shook her head slowly from side to side. She patted me absently on the shoulder and began steering her way over to my mother. I saw her engage my mother in serious conversation.

Later, when we were loading the presents into the trunk of Mother's car, I asked her what Neecy had been saying. Mother laughed.

"Well, if you really want to know—she asked me if it was really true that you were marrying a Yankee. I said, 'Well, Miss Neecy, he is from Ohio.' And she said, 'Poor Aida. I know you're worried. But there *are* some nice ones. Aurora will be all right, honey.'"

FIVE

NOW THAT I'D taken on renovating the Julius house—
I just couldn't think of it as the Zinsner house—the
time before the wedding flew by. I got the apartment
above the garage finished first. The carpet was laid
within three days after the painter finished the trim. I
cleaned the furniture I'd bought, positioned it inviti-
ingly, relined the kitchen shelves, cleaned the stove,
and made the bed. I'd gotten a set of china for four at
WalMart, and some wedding gift pots and pans I
didn't need went into the kitchen cabinets. I put towels in the bathroom, hung a shower curtain, and arranged some of the seashell soap in a soap dish. It
looked pretty and inviting and clean, and I hoped I'd
done Martin's friends proud.

The work on the big house went slower. Some of the
workmen I wanted were busy, and the carpet took
longer to come than it was supposed to, and I had a
hard time picking out paint and wallpaper. I was
frantic to have it finished; my townhouse and Mother's guest bedroom were overflowing with the wedding gifts and furniture I'd kept from Jane Engle's
house. Martin's furniture was still in storage at a
warehouse closer in to Atlanta, and I made a trip there
to see what he had. In between making decisions,

fretting over delays, and spending hours worrying, I had to get dressed appropriately and punctually for the remaining parties in our honor.

Now, these are all very pleasant problems to have, I know. But I did begin to get tired, and frayed, and desperate. Martin seemed unprecedently grim, too, though his bad mood didn't seem to have anything to do with the wedding.

So I was really glad to greet the Youngbloods when they arrived from Florida. I was at the Julius house when they drove in at noon one day about a week and a half before the wedding.

Angel Youngblood emerged from the dusty old Camaro first. Her legs swung out and out and out, and then the rest of her followed. I gaped. Angel was easily as tall as her husband. Muscular and sleek as a cheetah, she had pale blond hair gathered up in a ponytail. She was wearing the loose sheeting pants that weightlifters wear when they train, and a gray tank top. She had a broad, thin-lipped mouth, a straight nose, and brilliant blue eyes in a narrow face. She wore no makeup. She looked around her carefully, her eyes gliding right over me and then coming back to note me. We looked at each other curiously.

"I'm Aurora," I said finally, shaking her hand, which was an experience for both of us. "You must be Angel?"

"Yes," she said. "It's been a long drive. It's good to get out of the car."

She stretched, an impressive process that showed muscles I didn't even know women had.

Her husband came to stand beside her. He looked even swarthier, his face more pock-marked, against her smooth sleekness.

"Shelby, nice to see you again," I said.

"Aurora," he nodded.

The carpet layers, who were carrying in the pad, stopped to stare at Angel. Shelby looked at them. They hastily headed into the house.

It wasn't that she was pretty. She wasn't. And her chest was almost flat. She was just very obviously strong and fit and golden tan, and her hair was such a pretty color. It was really just like seeing a wild animal walk into the yard—beautiful and scary at the same time.

"Please come see the garage apartment," I said a little shyly. "I hope you like it." I turned to precede them up the steps. Suddenly I reconsidered. "No," I said, turning. "Here are the keys."

It was theirs, they should see it alone, without me there to make them feel that they had to admire it. I left to start overseeing the carpet layers.

About an hour later they came to the house, looking about them carefully, like cats examining a new environment.

While Shelby went upstairs at my invitation to finish the tour, Angel put a broad hand on my shoulder to get my attention. I looked up at her.

"It's the nicest place we've lived in years," she said unexpectedly. "Shelby told me what it was like before. Thank you for everything."

"You're welcome. If you want to change anything, now is the time, with all these home repair people coming in and out."

She looked at me blankly, as if changing her environment was an alien concept. "Where do you want us to park?"

"Since Martin and I don't have both cars here, just park in the garage. I don't know what we'll work out later after the wedding, but we'll think of something."

"Okay. We've carried our suitcases up, and we're ready to start work."

"Work" sounded more formal than the casual "helping you out" relationship Martin had suggested. But I certainly did need help.

"Let me tell you what I want to do here in the house, and how far I've gotten on each item," I began. To my surprise, she pulled a small ruled pad out of her pocket, and uncapped a pen clipped to it. Shelby was suddenly beside her, listening just as attentively as if I were updating them on a missile launch. Feeling nervous and awkward, I started explaining, room by room, the plans I'd made, and showed them the paint, wallpaper, and carpet samples for each room that I'd sorted into a divided accordian folder. In the section I'd accorded each room was also a list of necessary repairs or changes, and taped to the front was a list of things I had yet to do before we left on our honeymoon. This list included such things as "Start paper delivery. Order new return-address stickers. New library card. Box books in townhouse. New stove will be delivered Monday A.M., be there...." and it went on and on.

"I think we can take care of this," Shelby said after a thorough briefing.

"You do?" I know I sounded idiotic, but I was stunned. It had never occurred to me they'd take the whole thing off my hands.

"Of course we can't sign things for you," Angel said. "And you'll want to come see for yourself, at least once a day. I know I would. But I think we can make sure all this happens on time, and I see you've got a list of all the phone numbers we might need, taped here to the folder."

I am capable of organization.

"You'd do that?" I was still having trouble grasping the idea that relief was standing right before me.

"Of course," Angel said again, surprised in turn. "That's what we're here for."

"When will Shelby start work at Pan-Am Agra?"

"Oh, not until you all are back," Shelby said. "Martin wanted us to be sure everything kept on going while you were gone, and that's what Angel and I intend to do."

"Oh...that's wonderful. Thank you," I said from the bottom of my heart.

They both looked uncomfortable and glanced at each other.

"It's our job," Angel said, with a little shrug. A little shrug on Angel was a pretty large gesture.

I had to relax them before I left. "Now," I said briskly, "the carpenter building the bookshelves here in the hall is supposed to come this afternoon, but he'll get his wife to call with some excuse, about 12:30. So tell him that if he doesn't come in to finish the job, we'll hire someone else tomorrow."

"Okay," Shelby nodded. "And who will we call tomorrow? Or am I bluffing?"

"Bluffing. He'll come in today, but he just needs prodding. He likes to go fishing."

"So do I," Shelby said. "I feel for him. Well, go on if you have something else you need to be doing. We'll handle things here."

"Thank you," I said again, and I meant it just as much.

THAT EVENING we had scheduled another session with Aubrey. I got to St. James early, but Aubrey was already there, sitting on the steps of the church. He was watching the sun go down, a little ritual he liked to observe every now and then. I plopped down by him, glad to sit and let my brain rest for a little bit.

After our hellos, we slumped together companionably for a few minutes, thinking our separate thoughts, watching the splendor unfold to the west. Aubrey had a wonderful quality of restfulness, the inner relaxation of a man who is square with the world and its maker.

"Martin's not early, for once," Aubrey observed, after a while.

"No...guess he had a meeting."

"I think he usually comes early because he doesn't want to leave you alone with me."

"You think so?"

"Could be," Aubrey said neutrally.

"He knows I love him," I said.

"He knows other people love you."

I mulled that over.

"You're implying that he's extremely jealous?"

"Could be."

"Do you like Martin?"

"I admire him. He has many fine qualities, Roe. I don't think you'd pick a man who didn't. He's intelligent, strong, a leader. And he obviously loves you. But you're going to have to stand up to him on everything, every point, not let him get the upper hand. Once he has that, he won't be able to stop."

"This is a surprise, Aubrey." I watched an ant toiling across the gray concrete of the sidewalk.

"I care about you. Of course, I care about everyone in this congregation, but you're a special person to me, and you know it. In these counseling sessions, I've seen how much Martin loves you and how much you love him, and I've seen that both of you believe in God and are trying to lead a good life. But Martin feels he is a law to himself, that he and God are each autonomous.''

We were sitting with our knees almost in our faces because the steps were so shallow. I leaned my head down on my knees, felt their hard caps and the movement of my muscles underneath, the amazing way my body worked. I was trying not to feel scared.

''You'll perform the wedding?''

''Yes. And I'm not saying anything to you I won't say to Martin. I just wanted to talk to you because I felt I was being prevented from doing it. And because I'll always be fond of you.''

''Are you going to marry Emily?'' I was being impertinent, but the evening and the quiet of the neighborhood around the church encouraged intimacy.

''We're thinking about it. She hasn't been a widow very long, and her little girl is trying to understand her daddy's absence.'' Emily's husband had been killed in a wreck the year before, and she'd moved to Lawrenceton because she had an aunt living here.

Emily Kaye was dull as dishwater, but of course I wasn't going to say that to Aubrey. At least my intended was exciting.

And here he came in his Mercedes. Martin was groomed to a T even after a long day at work, his striped coat still crisp, his suit unwrinkled. My heart gave its familiar lurch at the sight of him, and I sighed involuntarily.

''You're really in love,'' Aubrey said very quietly, as if to reassure himself.

"Yes."

I smiled at Martin as he got out of the car and came toward us, and he didn't look jealous or even uneasy at Aubrey and me sitting tête-à-tête. But he pulled me up by my hands and gave me a kiss that lasted too long and was almost ferocious.

"I'll go unlock the office," Aubrey murmured, and rose from the steps.

"Your friends got in today," I told Martin.

"Shelby called me. What did you think of Angel?"

"I've never met anyone like her, or like Shelby, for that matter."

"What do you mean?" We began walking down the south sidewalk to the parish hall where Aubrey's office was, the dusk gathering around us. I could see the desk lamp shining through Aubrey's uncurtained window.

"Well," I said slowly and carefully, "they seem used to having very little, to needing very little." I was uncertain how to phrase my next thought. "They're very quick to understand your wishes and act on them, and they don't reveal anything about themselves, about what they want. Oh, gosh, that makes them sound like a maid and a butler, and they're anything but that. But do you see what I mean?"

He didn't answer for a moment, and I was afraid I'd offended him.

"They're very independent, and very capable of making quick judgment calls, Angel even faster than Shelby maybe," Martin said finally. "But I understand you. Shelby has never been one to talk about himself, and I was sure he'd marry someone who talked nonstop, but he married Angel. She'll tell you more about herself than Shelby will, but she isn't any chatterer."

"They're going to be a great help with getting the house finished," I said carefully, when it became apparent Martin wasn't going to volunteer any more—like, who were these people? Where had they come from, and what had they been doing there? Why were they willing to be in Lawrenceton, doing what they were doing here? "It's a relief knowing they're there."

"Great, honey. I wanted you to get some quiet time before the wedding. That house was running you ragged."

Ragged? I felt the urge to pop in the nearest women's room and stare into the mirror, suddenly terrified I'd see crow's feet and gray hair. Normally I am not morbidly self-conscious about my appearance, but the fittings for the wedding dress and the fuss over clothes in general for the past couple of months had made me very aware of how I looked.

"They took notes," I told Martin absently. "I think they'll do a great job."

"I want you to be happy," he said.

"I am," I told him, surprised. "I've never been happier in my life."

Then we were at the door to Aubrey's office, and we joined hands and went in. Our last session before the wedding, and Aubrey wasn't going to make it easy. He asked hard questions and expected honest answers. We had gone over what we expected from each other financially, emotionally, and in the matter of religion. And we had talked again about having children, with both of us unable to decide. Maybe indecision wasn't good, but it was better than holding opposing views. Right?

The counseling sessions had opened vistas of complexities I'd never imagined, the little and big adjustments and decisions of sharing life with another adult human being. It was the "working" aspect of marriage I'd somehow missed when my friends talked about their married lives. Martin, who was more experienced by reason of his previous marriage, had mentioned Cindy in the course of the sessions more than I'd ever heard him mention her before. Especially since I'd met Cindy, I listened carefully. And this evening, Aubrey asked Martin The Big Question.

"Martin, we've concentrated, naturally, on your relationship with Roe, since you're going to be married. But I wondered if you wanted to share your feelings about why your previous marriage didn't work out. Have we covered anything in these evenings together that rang any bells?"

Martin looked thoughtful. His pale brown eyes focused on the wall above Aubrey's dark head, his hands loosened the knot of his tie. "Yes," he said quietly, after a few seconds. "There were some things we never talked about, important things. Some things I liked to keep to myself. I don't like to think about the woman I love worrying about them."

My eyes widened. My mouth opened. Aubrey shook his head, very slightly. I subsided, but rebelliously. I would worry if I damn well chose to; I deserved the choice.

"But," Martin continued, "that wasn't the way the marriage could survive. Cindy ended up not trusting me about anything. She got sadder and more distant. At the time, I felt that if she had enough faith in me, everything would be okay, and I was resentful that she didn't have that faith."

"But now?" Aubrey prompted.

"I wasn't being fair to her," Martin said flatly. "On the other hand, she began to do things that were calculated to gain my attention ... flirt with other men, get involved with causes she had very little true feeling for..."

"And you didn't communicate these feelings to each other?"

"It was like we couldn't. We'd been talking so long about things like Barrett's grades, what time we had to be at the PTA meeting, whether we should install a sprinkler system, that we couldn't talk about important things very effectively. Our minds would wander."

"And now, in your marriage to Aurora?"

"I'll try." He glanced toward me finally, apologetically. "Roe, I'll try to talk to you about the most important things. But it won't be easy."

As we were leaving, Aubrey said, "I almost forgot, Roe. I was visiting a few members of the congregation who live in Peachtree Leisure Apartments yesterday. We were in that big common room in the middle, and an older lady came up to me and asked if I was the minister who was going to conduct the ceremony for your wedding."

"Who was she?"

"A Mrs. Totino. You know her? She said she'd read the engagement notice in the paper. She wanted to meet you."

"Totino," I repeated, trying to attach a face to the name. "Oh, I know! The Julius mother-in-law! I heard at the shower that she was still alive and living here, and I'd completely forgotten it."

"I never met her when I bought the house. Bubba Sewell ran back and forth with all the papers," Martin said.

"Is she in good health, Aubrey?" I asked.

"She seemed pretty frail. But she was full of vinegar and certainly all there mentally. The old gentleman I was visiting says she's the terror of the staff."

I pictured a salt-and-peppery little old lady who would say amusingly tart things the staff would quote to their families over supper.

"I'll go see her after the wedding," I said.

SIX

LATELY I'D BEEN feeling as if I were in one of those movies where calendar pages fly off the wall to indicate the passage of time. Events and preparations made the time blur. Only a few things stood out clearly when I thought about it later.

The night we were riding home from the barbecue Amina's parents held for us, out at their lake house, Martin finally told me where we were going on our honeymoon. He had asked what I wanted, and I had told him to surprise me. I had half-expected the Caymans, or perhaps a Caribbean cruise.

"I wanted you to have a choice, so I've made initial preparations for two things," he began, as the Mercedes purred down the dreadful blacktop that led to the state highway back into town. I leaned back against the seat, full of anticipation and barbecued pork.

"We can either go to Washington for two weeks, and do the Smithsonian right."

I breathed out a sigh of delight.

"Or we can go to England."

I was stunned. "Oh, Martin. But is there really something—I mean, both of those are things you would enjoy too?"

"Sure. I've been to the Washington area many times, but I've never had time to see the Smithsonian. And if you pick England, we can go on a walking tour of famous murder sites in London, if you'll come with me to get some suits made on Savile Row, or as close to Savile Row as I can manage."

"How can I pick?" I chewed on my bottom lip in happy agony. "Oh...England! I just can't wait! Martin, what a great idea!"

He was smiling one of his rare broad smiles. "I picked the right things, then."

"Yes! I thought for sure we'd be going to some island to lie on gritty sand and get all salty!"

He laughed out loud. "Maybe we can do that sometime, too. But I wanted you to have a really good time, and a beach honeymoon just didn't sound like you."

Once again, Martin had surprised me with his perception. If we'd sat down and consulted on it, I would never have thought of suggesting England (going farther than the Caribbean had never crossed my mind), and if I had, I would have dismissed the idea as something that wouldn't have appealed to Martin.

We had an absolutely wonderful time after we got to the townhouse.

ANOTHER MOMENT I remembered afterward was Amina's introduction to Martin. I was very excited about her meeting him and attributed her unusual silence thereafter to the bouts of nausea she was still experiencing. Amina, who had always been happily unconscious of her good health, was having a hard time adjusting to the new limits and discomforts her pregnancy was imposing on her. Her hair was hanging limply instead of bouncing and glowing, her skin was spotty, her ankles were swelling if she sat still for more than a short time, and she seemed to alternate nausea with heartburn. But every time she thought about the baby actually arriving, she was happy as a clam at high tide.

So at first I thought it was just feeling demoralized about her appearance that made Amina uncharacteristically silent. Finally, unwisely, I asked her directly what she thought about Martin.

"I know I'm not my normal self right now, but I'm not crazy, either," Amina began. I got that ominous feeling, the one you get when you know you're about to get very angry and it's your own fault. We were standing out in the front yard of the Julius house, which was beginning to look as my imagination had pictured it when I had first seen it. John Henry's legs, in their plumbers' overalls, were protruding from the crawl space under the house, a young black man was trimming the foundation bushes, and the Youngbloods were doing a strange Asian thing on the broad driveway in front of the garage. It was some kind of martial ballet alternating sudden kicks and screams with hissing breathing and slow graceful movements. Amina watched them for a moment and shook her head in disbelief. "Honey," she said, looking directly into my eyes, *"who are those people?"*

"I told you, Amina," I said, "Shelby is an old army buddy of Martin's, and he lost his job in Florida—"

"Cut the crap."

I gaped at my best friend.

"What job? Where, exactly? Doing what? And what does she do? Does she look like Hannah Housewife to you?"

"Well, maybe they're not exactly like the people we know..."

"Damn straight! Hugh said they looked more like people the criminal-law side of his firm would defend!"

Bringing in Hugh, her husband, was a mistake, Amina realized instantly. "Okay, okay," she said, holding up her hands, "truce. But listen, honey, those people seem very strange to me. Martin wanting them to live out here with you all—I don't know, it just looks...funny."

"Be a little more specific, Amina," I said very stiffly. "Funny? How?"

Amina shifted from foot to uncomfortable foot. "Could we sit down?" she asked plaintively. I recognized a delaying tactic, but she really was tired. I pushed a folding lawn chair in her direction. I pulled over one for myself. Martin and I had been sitting out on the lawn the evening before, looking at the house and talking about our plans.

"I shouldn't have started this," Amina muttered to herself and tried to arrange her altering body in the light aluminum-frame chair. "I'm just worried about you," she said directly. "If Martin was a regular guy in a regular job who came home every night, I'd like him fine. And I do like him as he is, because he obviously thinks you're the greatest thing since sliced bread. But he's gone so much, he works so hard, such long hours. Why does he have to be out of town so much? Plant managers are supposed to stay at the plant, right? And these Youngbloods." She shook her head.

"Amina, stop."

"Your mom's worried, too." She was crying.

The Youngbloods had finished their strange ritual and were doing some kind of exercise in which they faced each other, squatted, and whacked each other's arms.

My mother, I reflected, had been smart enough not to say anything.

To tell the truth, this conversation shook me.

I handed Amina a Kleenex from my shoulder bag.

"I'm just scared that—it almost looks like you'll be their prisoner."

"Amina, I think you need to go lie down," I said, after a little silence.

"Don't patronize me! I may be pregnant but I'm not stupid."

"Then you'll believe me when I say that I don't want to hear any more of this."

We each stared off angrily in opposite directions, composing ourselves, trying to be friends again.

It took a few days.

THE CEREMONY ITSELF was brief and beautiful. Lawrencetonians filled up my side of the church and half the rows on Martin's. Being older, and having moved so many times, Martin had not invited many people, and those who came were business associates from Pan-Am Agra, a few old friends from Ohio, and his sister Barbara. I had some sympathy for Barby since I'd learned more of her history while I was in Corinth, but still I knew she would never become my favorite person or my confidante. (She brought her daughter, a sophomore at Kent State, a pretty, dark, plump, young woman named Regina. Regina was not blessed with many brains and asked far too often why her cousin Barrett hadn't come to see his dad get married.)

So St. James Episcopal Church was full, Emily Kaye played the organ beautifully, my mother walked down the aisle with the dignity that was her trademark, Martin appeared from Aubrey's study with John at his side—Martin looked absolutely delicious in his tux—and Amina went down the aisle in her full-skirted dress that fairly well concealed her pregnancy. Then it was my turn.

My father and his wife had finally decided to come, pretty much at the last minute; you can imagine how their lack of enthusiasm made me feel. And then they'd left my brother Phillip with some friends in California.

My crushing disappointment had permanently altered the way I felt about my father.

I am no apple-cart upsetter. I am no flouter of tradition. And I am not a person who likes last-minute changes in plans. But when my father had arrived, I had told him I wanted to walk down the aisle by myself. My mother drew in a sharp breath, opened her mouth to say something, then looked at me and shut it. And I didn't explain my decision to Father, or wait for his reaction, or tell him not to get his feelings hurt. And Betty Jo had no say at all. So Father and Betty Jo had walked in before Mother.

That's why I came down the aisle by myself when Emily began playing the music I'd waited so many years to hear. I'd had my hair put up, I was wearing the earrings Martin had given me the night before we'd gotten engaged, I was wearing full bride regalia. I felt like the Homecoming Queen, Miss America, a Pulitzer Prize winner, and a Tony Award nominee, all rolled into one.

And we got married.

SEVEN

WE PULLED INTO our very own gravel driveway, groggy from the trip, glad to be home. I knew Martin had started thinking about the plant again, and I had been visualizing my own—our own—bed, and my washing machine, and staying in my nightgown until I was good and ready to get dressed. And my own coffee! Our honeymoon, which had been as sweet as honeymoons are supposed to be, had been wonderful, but I was really ready to be back in Lawrenceton. It was hard to believe we had to get through the rest of the day before going to bed. Martin had slept some on the airplane coming across the ocean, and I had too, but it wasn't especially restful sleep.

The house looked wonderful. The new carpet, paint, and the bookshelves were in. God bless the Youngbloods; they'd arranged the furniture I'd thought would be lined up against the walls. I'd left diagrams of how I wanted the bedrooms to be situated, but I hadn't been able to visualize the living room. It actually looked very nice, though I was sure I'd want to change a couple of things. Madeleine had already chosen a chair and mastered the pet door in the kitchen. Judging by her girth, the Youngbloods had been feeding her too well. She seemed faintly pleased to see me, and as always, totally ignored Martin.

In that distracted way people have when they come home from a trip and can't settle, we wandered separately around the house. Martin went to the large box of mail on the coffee table and began to sort through it—his pile, my pile—while I roamed through the dining room, noting all the wrapped presents on the table, to check out the kitchen. I'd moved most of my kitchen things here myself and gotten them in place before the wedding, and Martin's household goods had been retrieved from storage before the wedding, too, but there was a box or two yet to unpack; the essential things that I'd kept at my apartment until the day of the wedding. I'd have cleaned out the apartment and moved in with Mother if the furniture left me by Jane Engle hadn't already been taking up the third bedroom, and the second one had been promised to Barby Lampton for the week of the wedding.

I knew, catching sight of the back of Martin's head as I began to open the belated wedding presents stacked on the dining-room table, that I was going to experience an afterwedding slump, as we began the day-to-day part of our life together, so I was glad there was some work left to do on the house. I stared blearily at yet another set of wine glasses, and checked the box to see if they were from the Lawrenceton gift shop; they were. I could take them back tomorrow and trade them in on something we really needed, though what that might be, I didn't know, since it seemed to me we had enough things to last us our lifetimes.

The next package contained purple and silver placemats of such stunning hideousness that I had to call Martin to see them. We puzzled over the enclosed card together, and I finally deciphered the crabbed handwriting.

"Martin! These are from Mrs. Totino!"

"Mrs. who?"

"The mother-in-law! The one who found out they were all missing! Why has she sent us a present?"

"Probably glad to have the house off her hands after all these years."

"The money. I guess she's glad to have the money. The house did belong to her?" A sudden thought occurred to me. "Has the family been officially declared dead?"

"Not yet. Later this year, in a few months, in fact. The check to buy the house went into the estate. It was a strange house closing. Bubba Sewell represented the estate. Mrs. Totino, evidently, was appointed the conservator for the estate after a year. I don't think there are any other relatives."

I lifted one of the suitcases to take it upstairs. "I am headed for our own shower in our own bathroom with our own soap."

"And a nap in our bed?" he asked.

"Yep. Right after I call Mother and tell her we're back."

"Can I join you?"

"The phone call? The shower? The nap?"

"Maybe we can delay the phone call and work something in between the shower and the nap?"

"Could be," I said musingly. "But you'd better catch me quick, or the nap will claim me first."

"I don't know if I can move fast enough," Martin admitted, tucking the card back in the box with the placemats and walking through the living room to join me at the stairs, "but I can try."

He was fast enough. We inaugurated our new house in a very satisfactory manner.

AFTER A DAY to rest, Martin went happily to work, and I settled into the rest of my life. The downstairs bathroom hadn't been completed, and I had to harass a few people over that, but the upstairs had been finished and it was beautiful. Our bedroom was French blue, gray, and white; I'd used Martin's bedroom furniture in the guest room, and his bedspread had been maroon and navy, so I had worked those colors in there. The anonymous little room now housed Martin's exercise equipment and the clothes that couldn't fit in our closet. The wood of the stairs had been refinished and polished and the carpet that ran throughout the top floor ran down the stairs, too, a light blue.

When I'd had the carpet ripped up downstairs, I'd found the floors were all hardwood, and had had them refinished. There was a large oriental rug in the living room, another in the dining room, and a runner go-

ing down the hall. We'd turned the downstairs bedroom into an informal "family" sitting room. Martin's desk was in one corner, the television was in there,
and a couple of comfortable chairs grouped with tables and lamps.

Jane Engle's mother's antique dining-room table
and chairs now graced our dining room, and our living room was composed of things from Jane's, mine,
and Martin's households, an eclectic mix but one that
pleased the eye, I thought.

And the built-in bookcases lining the hall looked
wonderful. Any space not taken up by books was filled
with knickknacks we'd gotten as wedding presents, a
china bird here, a vase there. Two of Jane's bookcases—they were lawyer bookcases with wonderful
glass doors—were in the family room, and the rest of
the bookcases were in a storage lockup with some of
Martin's things, awaiting our final decision.

I wondered what had happened to the Julius family's belongings.

I was sitting at the butcher-block table in the
kitchen, drinking my coffee and trying to suppress the
desire for another piece of toast, when I saw Shelby
Youngblood coming down the stairs to the apartment. He walked around the far side of the garage and
I heard a car start. They must have decided that was
the most discreet place to park. He backed out, used
the concrete turnaround apron, and left (I presumed)
for work. His car crunched as it hit the gravel; sooner
or later we would have to have the rest of the drive-

way paved. I thought about Angel Youngblood in her peach and green apartment, and I remembered what Amina had blurted out before the wedding. Amina's concern had stuck to me like a cockleburr, irritating and hard to dislodge.

I found myself wondering what Angel would do with herself all day. It wasn't really any of my business; but I am curious about people around me. They're what I use to keep myself entertained.

I put the breakfast dishes in the dishwasher, wiped the counters, and went upstairs to get dressed. After wearing all my new "honeymoon" clothes, it was nice to get back into my oldest blue jeans and my mystery bookstore T-shirt. I did put on some makeup, so as not to give Martin too complete a shock when he came home today. I had picked out my red-framed glasses to wear and was brushing my hair and planning my day when I heard a double rap on the kitchen door.

Angel was wearing one of those spandex exercise outfits that practically outline your arteries and veins. This bra-and-shorts combination was in a striking black and pink flame design. She had a warmup jacket on over the bra. Her legs were long columns of muscle ending in heavy pink socks and black running shoes.

"Welcome back," she said briefly.

"Come in."

"Just for a minute."

"Thanks for arranging all the furniture."

She shrugged and managed a smile. It suddenly dawned on me that Angel was shy.

"I just dropped by before my run to tell you that later, when you're ready, I can come help you move the living-room stuff into the position you want. We just kind of put it to where it looked like a real room, but I figured you would want to rearrange when you got home." Angel had to look down and down at me, but she didn't seem either to mind or to feel it gave her an edge.

"Angel, what are you exactly?"

"Huh?"

"Are you my employee? Martin's employee, like Shelby? If so, what's your job description? I feel like I'm missing something."

I hoped I wasn't being rude, but it made me feel uneasy, her doing me all these favors, since she wasn't a personal friend. If she was getting paid for it, that was another matter.

That proved to be the case.

"Martin pays Shelby and me," she answered after looking at me consideringly for a moment. "Of course, Shelby gets a paycheck from the plant, but we get some money besides. For helping you all out here. Because this house is a little far from town, out of earshot . . . and Martin's gone a lot, Shelby tells me."

"Sit down, please." We faced each other over the table. "What does helping me out include?"

"Ah . . . well. Working in the yard, this is a lot of yard to keep trimmed and mowed and planted. And if you need heavy things done in the house. And to house-sit when you go somewhere and Martin's gone, too... like that."

We regarded each other intently. This was very interesting. What on earth had this woman's life been like?

"Thanks, Angel," I said finally, and she shifted a little in her chair. "Have a good run." She rose without haste, nodded, and drifted to the kitchen door, which opened onto the backyard.

"I'll be thinking about the living room while you run, and maybe later after you shower and everything, you could come over."

"Sure," she said, sounding relieved. "Should be about an hour, maybe a little longer."

"Fine." And I closed the door behind her, leaned against it, and wondered what she hadn't told me.

AT THE END OF a morning spent moving heavy objects, I knew a little more about Angel. She and Shelby had been married for seven years. They had worked together on their previous job. What that job was, was vague. I am southern enough to have trouble asking direct questions; I'd used up my quota for the day that morning in the kitchen. And Angel, whether deliberately or not, did not respond to anything but flat-out bald-faced directness. I still had no clear fix on her character.

Martin had a lunch meeting that day, and Mother was taking some clients out, so I sat down at the kitchen table and worked out a meal plan for the week, which was one of the things I'd heard good house-wives did, and shopped at the grocery accordingly. I'd cooked for Martin before, of course, and he'd grilled meat for us many times, but this would be the first meal I'd cooked for him as his wife in our new home, and I thought it should be fancy, but not so fancy that he got inflated ideas about what our daily cuisine would be: and also not so difficult that I ruined it. We'd gotten at least five cookbooks as wedding pres-ents, and I mildly looked forward to our eating our way through them.

I sat in our little family room and watched the news, reading through our backlog of magazines during the ads. Then I wrote some more thank-you's, managing to acknowledge over half the gifts that had arrived in our absence. When I walked to the end of the drive to put the notes in the mailbox, I noticed for the first time that the Youngbloods had put up their own mailbox. That made sense, since we had the same ad-dress; it was a problem I hadn't thought of before, and here it was already solved. I ambled back up the drive, looking idly through the load of bills and occupant notices and free samples I'd found in the box. As we'd decided in our premarital counseling, I would be re-sponsible for paying the month-to-month bills from our joint account, into which Martin and I each de-posited a predetermined amount from our separate incomes. So I pulled out our brand-new joint checkbook, paid the bills, and signed the checks "Aurora Teagarden."

Okay, okay. I'd kept my name, that absurd and ridiculous name that had been my bane my whole life. When it got right down to it, I just couldn't become anyone else. Martin had had a hard time about that, but I had a gut feeling I was right. When I feel like that, I am fairly immovable. And I can't tell you how much better it made me feel. I had my own money, I had my own friends and family, I had my own name. I was one lucky woman, I told myself as I sliced strawberries.

Martin opened the front door and yelled gleefully, "Hi, honey! I'm home!"

I started laughing.

I was actually able to turn from the sink and say, "Hello, dear. How did your day go?" just like a sitcom mom.

I was one lucky, uneasy woman.

EIGHT

THE NEXT MORNING, on a whim, I went to Peachtree Leisure Apartments, a sort of independent old folks' home, as Neecy Dawson had so cheerfully pointed out. I'd been there before to visit various people, but not in a long time. There'd been a few changes. Before, there'd been a directory in the large lobby, and you could just walk in and take the elevator to the floor you needed. Now, there was a very large black man with a narrow mustache seated at the desk, and the directory was gone. There was a television camera pointed from one corner that embraced almost the whole lobby area.

"They was getting robbed," the man explained when I asked about the change. "People was coming in here, reading a name and apartment number, and just wandering through the building till they found who they wanted. They'd sell them magazines the old people didn't need, if they thought the old person was senile enough, or they'd just rob them if the old folks were feeble. So now I am here. And at night, from five until eleven, there's another man. Now, who did you come to see?"

Somewhat shaken at this picture he painted of wolves roaming the halls in Peachtree Leisure Apartments, I told him I'd come to see Mrs. Melba Totino.

"She expecting you, Miss?"

"Mrs. No, Ms." What was I going to call myself? He was eyeing me warily. "No, Mrs. Totino isn't expecting me. I just came to thank her for the wedding present."

"She *gave* you something?" The brown eyes widened in a burlesque of surprise. "You *must* be a friend."

"I take it this is unusual?"

But after his little joke, he wasn't going to say anything else.

"I'll call her, if you just wait a minute," he said.

He picked up the phone, dialed, and told Melba Totino about my presence in the lobby. She would see me.

"Go on up," he said. "She don't get too many visitors."

The elevator smelled like a doctor's office, like rubbing alcohol and disinfectant and cold steel. The guard had told me there was a physician's assistant actually in residence, and of course a doctor on call. There was a cafeteria in the building for those who "enrolled" for that service, and groceries could be delivered from one of the local stores. Everything was very clean, and the lobby had been dotted with old people who at least looked alert and comfortable, if not exactly happy. I supposed, if you couldn't live entirely on your own, this would be a good place to live.

Mrs. Totino's apartment was on the third floor. I could tell by the spacing of the doors that some apartments were larger than others. Hers was one of the small ones. I knocked, and the door swung open almost before I could remove my hand.

I could look her straight in the eyes, so she wasn't more then five feet tall. Her eyes were dark brown, sunk in wrinkles that were themselves blotched with age spots. She had a large nose and a small mouth. Her wispy white hair was escaping from a small bun on the back of her head. She wore no glasses, which surprised me. Her ludicrously cheerful yellow and orange striped dress was covered with a gray sweater and the air that rushed out smelled strongly of air freshener, talcum powder, and cooking.

"Yes?" Her voice was deep and pleasant, not shaky as I'd expected.

"I'm Aurora Teagarden, Mrs. Totino."

"That's what Duncan said. Now, what kind of name is Duncan for a black man? I ask you." And she backed into her apartment to indicate I should enter. "I asked him that, too," she said with great amusement at her own daring. "I said, 'I never heard no black man called Duncan before.' He said, 'What you think I should be called, Miz Totino? LeRoy?' That Duncan! I laughed and laughed."

Who-wee, what a knee-slapper. I bet Duncan had thought so, too.

"Have a seat, have a seat."

I looked around me nervously. There were seats to be had, but everything was so busy I wasn't sure if they were occupied or not. The sofa and matching chair were violently flowered in orange and brown and cream. The table between the chair and the sofa contained a *TV Guide,* the ugliest lamp in the universe, a red-and-white glass dish containing hard candy, a pair of reading glasses, a box of Kleenex, and a stunningly sentimental figurine of a little girl with big eyes petting a cuddly puppy with the legend across the base, "My Best Friend." I finally decided one of the couch cushions was empty and lowered myself gingerly down.

"This apartment building is very nice," I offered.

"Oh, yes, the new security makes all the difference in the world! Can I get you a cup of coffee? I'm afraid I only have instant decaffeinated."

Then why have coffee at all? "No, thank you."

"Or a—Coke? I think I have a Coke stuck in the refrigerator."

"Okay, thanks."

She walked bent over, and haltingly. In the jammed tiny room there were two doorways, one at the rear left leading into the kitchen and one at the right into the bedroom. I heard the sounds of fumbling and muttering in the kitchen and took the chance to look around me.

The walls were covered with doodads of every description. Gold-tone butterflies in a group of three, one rather pretty painting of a bowl of flowers, two awful prints of cherubic children being sweet with cute animals, a straw basket holding dried flowers that looked extremely dusty, a plaque with The Serenity Prayer... I began to feel dazed at the multitude of things that presented themselves for inspection. I thought of all the room in our house and felt a stir of guilt.

Then the television caught my attention. All this time it had been on, but I had not paid any attention to the picture. I realized now that the scene I was seeing was the apartment building lobby. An old ma with a walker moved slowly across the screen as I watched. Good Lord. I wondered if many of the residents chose to watch life in their lobby.

Mrs. Totino tottered back into the room with a glass of Coke and ice clutched in her shaking hand. The ice was tinkling against the glass with a quick tempo that was distinctly nerve-wracking.

"Did you like the placemats?" Mrs. Totino asked suddenly and loudly.

We negotiated the transfer of the Coke from her hand to mine.

"I've never seen any like them," I said sincerely.

"Now, I know you won't be offended when I tell you that they were wedding presents for T.C. and Hope. They'd been packed away in a drawer for these many years, and I thought, why not let someone else enjoy them? And they've never been used—it's not like I gave you a *used* gift!"

"Recycled," I suggested.

"Right, right. Everything's this recycling now! I recycled them."

I had hoped to see a picture of the Julius family, but in all this clutter, there were only two photographs, in a double frame balanced precariously on the television set. Both photographs were very old. One showed a stern small woman with dark hair and eyes standing stiffly beside a somewhat taller man with lighter hair and a thin-lipped shy face. They were wearing clothes dating from somewhere around the twenties, I thought. In the other picture, two girls who strongly resembled each other, one about ten and the other perhaps twelve, hugged each other and smiled fixedly at the camera.

"Me and my sister, her name's Alicia Manigault, isn't that a pretty name?" Mrs. Totino said fondly. "I've always hated my name, Melba. And the other picture is the only one ever taken of my parents."

"Your sister is still . . . does she live close?"

"New Orleans," Mrs. Totino said. "She has a little house in Metairie, that's right by New Orleans." She sighed heavily. "New Orleans is a beautiful place, I envy her. She never wants to come see me. I go there every now and then. Just to see the city."

I wondered why she didn't just move. "You have relatives here now, Mrs. Totino?"

"No, not since . . . not since the tragedy. Of course you know about that."

I nodded, feeling definitely self-conscious.

"Yet you bought the house, or your husband bought it for you, I understand from Mr. Sewell."

"Yes, ma'am."

"You aren't scared? Other people backed down from buying it at the last minute."

"It's a beautiful house."

"Not haunted, is it? I don't believe in that stuff," said Mrs. Totino robustly. I looked surreptitiously for a place to deposit my glass. The Coke was flatter than a penny on a railroad track.

"I don't either."

"When that lawyer with the stupid name called to say someone really wanted to buy it, and he said it was a couple about to be married, I thought, I'll just send them a little something...after all these years, the house will be lived in again. What kind of shape was it in?"

So I told her about that, and she asked me questions, and I answered her, and all the while she never talked about what I was most interested in. Granted, the disappearance of her daughter, her granddaughter, and her son-in-law had to have been dreadful, but you would think she would mention it. Aside from that stiff reference to "the tragedy" she didn't bring it up. Of course she was most interested in changes we had made to the apartment over the garage, the one built for her, the one she'd inhabited such a short time. Then she moved to the house, conversationally. Had we repainted? Yes, I told her. Had we reroofed? No, I told her, the real estate agent had ascertained that Mr.

Julius had had a new roof put on when he bought the house.

"He came here to be near relatives?" I asked carefully.

"His relatives," she said with a sniff. "His aunt Essie never had any children, so when he retired from the Army, he and Charity moved here to be close to her. He'd saved for years to start his own business, doing additions onto houses, carpentry work, stuff he'd always wanted to do. He could have gone anywhere he wanted, but he picked here," she said gloomily.

"And asked you to live with them?"

"Yes," she admitted. "Want some more Coke? There's half a can left in the kitchen. No? Yes, they had figured out how they could add an apartment on the garage. Didn't want me in the house with 'em. So I moved from New Orleans—I'd been sharing a place with my sister—and came up here. Left her down there." She shook her head. "Then this all happened."

"So," I said, about to ask something very nosy but unable to stop myself, "why did you stay?"

"Why?" she repeated blankly.

"After they disappeared. Why did you stay?"

"Oh," she said with comprehension. "I get you. I stayed here in case they turned up."

"DON'T YOU THINK that's kind of eerie, Martin?" I asked that night, as he put away the leftovers and I washed the dishes.

"Eerie? Sentimental, maybe. They're obviously not going to turn up alive, after all these years."

I recalled the saccharine pictures in the apartment, the figurine. All very sentimental. "Maybe so," I conceded reluctantly.

"Did you see that Angel and I had rearranged the living room?" I asked after a moment. I squeezed out my sponge and pulled the plug. The sink water drained out with a big gurgle, like a dragon drinking water.

"It looks good. I think the gallery table Jane left you needs some work, though. One of the legs is loose."

"I think maybe you'd better tell me about the Youngbloods, Martin."

"I told you, Shelby needed a job..."

I gathered my courage. "No, Martin, tell me really."

He was hanging up the dishtowel on a rack mounted beside the sink. He got it exactly straight.

"I wondered when you were going to ask," he said finally.

"I wondered when you were going to tell."

He turned to face me and leaned against the counter. I leaned against the one at a right angle to him. I crossed my arms across my chest. His sleeves were rolled up and his tie was loosened. He crossed his arms across his chest, too. I wondered what a body-language expert would make of this.

"Are the Youngbloods my jailers? Are they here to keep an eye on me?" I thought I'd lead off with the most obvious question.

Martin swallowed. My heart was pounding as if I'd been running.

"I knew Shelby in Vietnam," he began. "He helped me get through it."

I nodded, just to show I was registering this information.

"After the war...after our part of the war...I'd met some intelligence people in Vietnam. I spoke some Spanish already, and so did Shelby. We had some Hispanic guys in our unit and we spoke Spanish with them, got a lot better. It was something to do."

Martin's knuckles were white as he gripped his crossed arms.

"So, after we left Nam, we left the Army but we signed on with another company that was really the government."

"You were asked?"

"Yes." His eyes met mine for the first time, the pale brown eyes edged with black lashes and brows that were Martin's most immediately striking feature. "We were asked. And in our—working with us, was Jimmy Dell Dunn, a swamp boy from Florida who'd grown up next to some exiled Cubans. His Spanish was even better than ours." Martin half-smiled and shook his head at some fleeting memory of a time and place I couldn't even imagine.

"What we did was," he resumed, "sell guns. Really, we were giving them away. But it was supposed to seem like we were an independent company selling them. What can I say, Roe? I thought, at least in the beginning, that I was doing something good for my country. I never made any personal profit. But it's become harder and harder to know who the good guys are." He was looking out the window into the night. I wondered if the Youngbloods could look outside the side window of their apartment and down into our kitchen. I could not move to draw the curtain.

And Martin had his own private view of darkness.

Guns. Guns were better than drugs. Right? Of course with all Martin's trips to South America, I had been worried Martin's pirate side had led him into the dangerous and lucrative drug trade, though Martin had often expressed profound contempt for those who used drugs and those who sold them. Guns were better.

"And we delivered them, in some very remote places, to right-wing groups. Some of these people were okay, some were crazy. They were all very tough. A few were just—bandits."

I pulled my glasses off and rubbed my eyes with my hand. I had a headache. I put them back on and pushed them up on my nose with a finger. I stared past Martin's arm. I needed to get some Bon Ami and really scrub that sink.

"And one day—it was about midmorning, we were up in the Chama Mountains...we were making a delivery to one of the better guys. Out of nowhere, we were ambushed by another group who'd heard somehow about the delivery. I got the scar on my shoulder, Shelby got a worse wound in the leg. And Jimmy Dell got his head blown off."

I took in my breath quickly. I was married to a man who had witnessed this barbarity, this horror, had been part of it. I began to shiver. I wanted this story over.

"Shelby and I got out of there, just barely. We had to leave Jimmy Dell, and he was our pilot. Shelby knew enough about the copter to get us out, though he was bleeding like a stuck pig. And then it took us a while to heal. We heard the group we were supposed to take the guns to were all dead before we got there. When we came back to the States, Shelby went to see Jimmy Dell's family in Florida. Jimmy Dell had been the oldest kid by far, and there were five more after him. The youngest one was Angel. She was too young then, Shelby thought, and Mr. Dunn surely thought so, too. So Shelby wandered for a while."

And Martin had gone to stay on that isolated farm in Ohio with a man he hated, just to have a familiar place to recover. And while he was there, he hooked back up with Cindy. And they married. And he never told her this. Or not all of it. Ridiculously, I could not stop shivering.

"After a few years Shelby went back to Florida. Angel had gotten interested in martial arts in high school after something happened to her, and she got Shelby interested, too. They got married, and they began working as a team of bodyguards."

Gee, I wondered whom you would work for in southern Florida.

"But they didn't want to work for that kind." My face must have spoken for me. "So later, mostly they worked at the smaller movie studios up and down the East Coast, guarding people who were there temporarily. Some of the people were pretty famous." Martin attempted a smile. "And they did some stunts in karate movies, too. Their last job was for a woman who told Shelby she owed a lot of money to the wrong people.

"She didn't owe it, Roe." Martin looked directly at me. "She'd stolen it, and they found her. They let the Youngbloods live, but they gave them a beating they'd remember. Angel was in the hospital, still, when Shelby came up here to find me. In their line of work, you can't get insurance, and they were broke, and they needed to leave the area for a while. I'd been worried about you being out here by yourself when I was out of town, and the apartment being empty... you're shaking."

He came over to me in two steps, waited a moment to see if I would hit him if he touched me, then put his arms around me. I felt his heavy muscles encircle me, and I had the stray thought that the workouts I had attributed to a desire to stay fit and look good were actually aimed toward keeping him ready for self-defense. I lay my head against his thick chest and let some of the shaking be absorbed by him.

"So," he said to the top of my hair, almost in a whisper, "what's going to happen now?"

"I'm going to get some Bon Ami and scrub the sink."

Martin held me away from him. He was angry. "I'll go in the family room and work until you feel like talking."

He left the kitchen through the hall door, his shoes making little noises on the hardwood as he crossed the hall.

I got the Bon Ami and a sponge with a rough scrubbing side, and set to work. I thought of a conversation I'd had with my mother. We'd been talking about love, and she'd said that women who stay with men who damage them have some deep need to be damaged; they can't possibly love the damager, that can't be the reason they stay. A woman with a strong sense of self-preservation will leave the bad relationship to save herself; the self-preservation will kill the love, so the individual will leave and be saved from further harm. My mother had cited herself: When my father had begun to be unfaithful, she had left, and she no longer loved him.

I loved Martin so much it made me catch my breath, sometimes. He had not told me the whole truth. I was going to stay. I had no idea what he was thinking, sitting there in our new room in our new house.

I rinsed the Bon Ami out of the sink. It was gleaming. It had probably never been so clean in its entire existence.

I seemed unable to string a coherent chain of thought together. I was relieved beyond measure that it hadn't been drugs. I would have had to leave. Guns were bad. Could I live with guns? I could live with the guns. And why on earth had Martin fallen in love with me, anyway? It was like a mating between a Martian and a Venusian. I doubled over and put my head on my arms on the counter and began to cry.

Martin heard and came in. He hated it when I cried. He turned me around and held me, and this time I pressed against him, hard, as though I were trying to crawl inside his skin. After a few moments, this had the inevitable effect, even under the emotional circumstances. Martin moved restlessly, and I kept my arms wrapped around him and raised my face to his.

NINE

MARTIN LEFT for work the next morning still eyeing me warily but apparently relieved that I was quietly working on whatever reaction his revelations had raised.

I watched him walk to the garage. I had the window open to let in the cool morning air, so I heard him tell Madeleine in no uncertain terms to get off the hood of his Mercedes. Martin was so fond of his car that he would not leave it parked at the airport when he had to catch a plane, but instead invariably took one of the company cars, so the cat was living dangerously. Madeleine sauntered insolently out of the garage as Martin backed out, reversed on the concrete apron, and took off down the gravel. I went out with the bag of cat food and filled her bowl. She rewarded me with a perfunctory purr. I sat on the steps in my bathrobe and watched her eat every bit of kibble.

I went through the rest of my little morning rituals in the same numb way. I'd been faced with something so bizarre it was just going to take me a little time to assimilate it. I thought of the men some of my classmates had married: a hardware store owner, an insurance salesman, a farmer, a lawyer. My dating a police officer had been thought very exotic by my friends. Police officers were too close to the wormy side of life, the side we didn't see because we didn't turn rocks over.

For whatever reason.

From our beautiful triple bedroom windows that looked out over our front yard, and across the road, to rolling fields, I spied Angel Youngblood going out for her morning run. This time she was wearing solid gold. She did her stretches, in itself an impressive sight, and then she began to run. I watched her lope down the driveway and out onto the road, long legs pumping in rhythm, blond ponytail bouncing. Angel was energetic. Soon she would be bored.

I had an idea.

I was watching for her when she came back, and when I figured she'd had time to shower and dress, I called her. I'd found their number written on the pad by the telephone on Martin's desk when I'd gone to make an errand list the day before.

"Angel," I said after she answered. "If you wouldn't mind coming over after you've run whatever errands you need to run, I have a project."

THAT MORNING I grasped the true beauty of the concept of having an employee. Angel and I didn't know each other, were bound by no ties of friendship or kin or community, but she was bound to help me achieve my goal.

And since Angel was an employee, she had to help me without protest. She had come over in blue jeans and a T-shirt and sneakers, looking like a healthy farm girl who tossed bales of hay up to the loft with her bare hands. I had braided my hair to keep it out of the way. I had assembled a retractable metal tape measure, a pad and pencil, and a copy of the most comprehensive newspaper article dealing with the Julius's family disappearance. I'd had that stuck away in a file for years, since I'd thought of doing a presentation on it for the Real Murders Club.

I intended, of course, to find the Julius family.

I handed the article to Angel and waited till she read it.

Police continued their search for the T.C. Julius family, reported missing yesterday morning by Mrs. Julius's mother, Melba Totino.

Mrs. Totino called the police after walking across to the family home from her adjacent garage apartment Saturday morning and finding no one at home. After some hours of waiting, and the discovery that the family car and truck were still in the garage, Mrs. Totino reported the disappearance.

Missing are T.C. Julius, a retired army sergeant who had hoped to open a business locally; his wife, Hope; and their daughter Charity, 15. Julius is described as 5-11, 185 pounds, 46, with graying brown hair and blue eyes. Hope Julius has dark brown hair, blue eyes, is 5-4 and 100 pounds. She is 42 years old, and is suffering from cancer. Charity Julius, who had just begun attending the Lawrenceton High School, has blue eyes and shoulder length brown hair. She is approximately 5-4 and 120 pounds.

The Juliuses had moved to Lawrenceton four months ago to be close to Mr. Julius's only surviving relative, his aunt, Essie Nyland. Mrs. Nyland is described by friends as being distraught at the disappearance. "She'd been so happy at T.C. moving here, since she's in poor health," said one neighbor, Mrs. Lyndower Dawson. "I'm afraid this will finish her."

The day before the disappearance appeared to be a normal one, Mrs. Totino told local authorities. She reported spending most of the day in her own apartment and joining the family for meals, as usual. She said Harley Dimmoch, a friend of Charity Julius's from their previous hometown of Columbia, S.C., visited the family. He left before dark, having spent the day helping Mr. Julius around the house.

In the late afternoon, local contractor Parnell Engle arrived to pour the concrete for a new patio T.C. Julius had planned at the rear of the house. He saw and spoke to Hope and Charity Julius, who both seemed normal at that time.

Detective Jack Burns describes his department as "pursuing all leads with the utmost vigor."

"It doesn't look as though they left volun- tarily, since the family vehicles are still in the ga- rage," he commented. *"On the other hand, there are no signs of violence and all their possessions are still here."*

He urged any resident who has knowledge of the Julius family to call the police station imme- diately.

There were pictures with the article: a shot of the house and a studio portrait of the family. T.C. Julius was a sturdy man with an aggressive smile and a square face. His wife, Hope, looked thin, frail, and ill, shrunken to the same size and frame as their teenage daughter. Charity Julius had shoulder-length hair that turned under neatly and an oval face like her moth- er's. She wasn't a pretty girl, but she was attractive, and she held herself like a girl who's used to being a force to reckon with.

"THAT'S THIS HOUSE," Angel commented, studying the picture. She checked the date at the top of the ar- ticle. "Over six years ago."

"Where do you think they are?" I asked.

"I think they're dead," she answered without hesi- tation. "He just moved here. He was going to open a new business. No mention of trouble in the marriage. No mention of the daughter getting into trouble with the law. He'd just built the apartment for the mother- in-law, so he must have been able to tolerate her. No apparent reason for him to do a flit, especially taking the wife and daughter with him.''

"I think they're still here. The car was still here.''

"But the killer could have taken them away in his or her own car,'' Angel objected reasonably. "What if the Dimmoch boy took them away and dumped them on the way home?''

"Then why haven't the bodies turned up?''

"Not found yet. They haven't found Hoffa, have they?''

I would not be daunted. "I just think with the car here, with the bodies not having been found elsewhere, that the chances are good they're here somewhere.''

"So, what do you want us to do?''

"I want us to measure every wall and floor and anything else we can think of.''

"You don't think the police did all that?''

"I don't know what they did, and I'm not sure I can find out. But I'll try. This is just step one.''

"Step one. Huh.'' She thought about it for a second and shrugged. "Where do we start?''

"The apartment, I'm afraid.''

"But the mother-in-law, Totino, says she was in the apartment all day. Or at least most of the day,'' Angel amended, checking the story again.

"So we start with the least likely and eliminate that,'' I said.

Angel looked at me consideringly. "Okay," she said, and we gathered our paraphernalia and started to work.

We were halted after an hour and a half by the arrival of Susu Hunter, who had been my friend my whole life. She hollered from the front porch.

"Roe! I know you're here somewhere!"

Angel and I extracted ourselves from the toolshed at the back of the garage, dusty and warm and fairly covered with cobwebs. The toolshed was an area I had overlooked during my house renovation. You could tell Mr. Julius had intended to use it often: There was pegboard lining the walls with hooks still protruding, and a workbench with a powerful fluorescent light overhead had been added. He had also altered the doors, apparently: They were extra-wide doors that swung back completely. Now it held some boxes of tools Martin had apparently not opened since he had been transferred to Chicago and lived in an apartment instead of a house. The boxes were keeping company with a lawnmower whose pedigree I could not figure out; perhaps it had been Jane Engle's. Assorted rakes, hoes, shovels, a sledgehammer, and an ax filled out our tool repertoire. Everything was grimy.

So, as I say, when Angel and I emerged, we weren't at our best.

"Look at you, Roe!" Susu said in some amazement. "What on earth have you been doing?"

"Rearranging the garage," I said, not untruthfully. We had a done a certain amount of straightening since we were in there already. "Susu, this is Angel Youngblood, a new arrival to Lawrenceton."

Susu said warmly, "We're so glad to have you here! I hope you like our little town. And if you don't have a church home yet, we'd just love to have you at Calgary Baptist."

I wished I had a camera tucked in my pocket. Angel's face was a picture. But underneath the gritty life she'd led in the past few years, Angel Dunn Youngblood was a true daughter of the South. She rallied.

"Thank you. We like it here very much so far. And thanks so much for inviting us to your church, but right now Shelby and I are very interested in Buddhism."

I turned to Susu in anticipatory pleasure.

"How fascinating!" she exclaimed, without missing a beat. "If you ever have a free Wednesday noon, first Wednesday in the month, we'd love to have you come speak at the Welcome to Town Luncheon."

"Oh. Thanks so much. Excuse me now, I'm expecting Shelby to come home to eat in half an hour or so." And Angel retired gracefully, bounding up the stairs to their apartment. I was relieved to see a little smile—a nonmalevolent smile—on her thin lips as she shut the door behind her.

"What an interesting woman," Susu said with careful lack of emphasis.

"She really is," I said sincerely.

"How on earth did she come to be living in your garage apartment?"

We began to stroll toward the house. Susu looked pretty, and a few pounds heavier than she'd been the year before. She'd just had her hair done in a defiant blond, and she was wearing sky blue polka-dotted slacks with a white shirt.

"Oh, her husband is a friend of Martin's."

"Is he any bigger than her?"

"A little."

"No children, I guess?"

"No…"

"Because I hate to think what size baby they'd have."

I laughed, and we began to talk about Susu's "babies," Little Jim and Bethany. Bethany was heavily involved in tap dancing, and Little Jim, the younger by a couple of years, was up to his brown belt in Tae Kwan Do.

"And Jimmy?" I asked casually. "How's he doing?"

"We're going to family therapy," Susu said in the voice of one determined not to be ashamed. "And though it's early to tell, Roe, I really think it's going to do us some good. We just went along for too long ignoring how we were really feeling, just scraping the surface to keep everything looking good for the people around us. We should have been more concerned about how things really were with us."

What an amazing speech for Susu Saxby Hunter to have made. I gave her a squeeze around the shoulders. "Good for you," I said inadequately and warmly. "I know if you both try, it'll work."

Susu gave me a shaky smile and then said briskly, "Come on! Show me this dream house of yours!"

Susu's dream house was the one her parents had left her, the one her grandparents had built. No house would ever measure up to it in her sight, and she was fond of dismissing our friends' new homes in new subdivisions as "houses, not homes!" But she pronounced this house a real home.

"Does it ever give you the creeps?" she asked with the bluntness of old friends.

"No," I said, not surprised she'd asked. Old friends or not, quite a lot of people had asked me that one way or another. "This is a peaceful house. Whatever happened."

"I'll bet sometimes you just wonder where they are."

"You're right, Susu. I do. I wonder that all the time."

Susu gave a theatrical shudder. "I'm glad it's yours and not mine," she said. "Can I smoke?"

"No, not inside. Let's sit out on the porch. I have one ashtray to go out there on the porch furniture."

There was now a swing attached to the roof of the porch, and some pretty outside chairs arranged in a circle including the swing. There were two or three small tables available, and I found an ashtray for Susu to use.

While we sat and talked of this and that, Shelby Youngblood pulled into the driveway and waved as he emerged from his car. We waved back and he ran up the stairs to his apartment to his Angel.

"Wow, he is big," Susu commented. "Not a looker, is he?"

"I think he is," I said, surprising myself.

"And you're the woman married to Hunk of the Year."

"Shelby is attractive," I said firmly. "I may be married, but I'm not blind."

"All those acne scars!"

"Just make him look lived-in."

"Does Martin come home for lunch?"

"So far, no. But he's still catching up from the time we spent away."

"Jimmy had Rotary today. Let's go in the kitchen and scrounge around for lunch."

We ate ham sandwiches and grapes and potato chips, and talked about my honeymoon and the latest meeting of the Ladies' Prayer Luncheon. My old friend Neecy Dawson had objected to the guest speaker's theology in loud, persistent terms, casting the ladies into a turmoil, and causing not a few of them to express the opinion it was time Neecy met God face to face.

"She was a friend of Essie Nyland's, wasn't she?" I asked casually.

"Neecy? Yep. Essie was a good friend of my grandmother's, too, outlived her by twenty years, I guess. Miss Essie died . . . what? Six years ago now, must be. Neecy's still going strong. She still knows everyone in this town, what they've done, and when they did it."

It struck me that I could have a profitable conversation with Miss Neecy. She'd told me of the arguments between the Zinsners when they built this house. It was that conversation that had given me the idea that there might be several hidey-holes the bodies of the Julius family could be in. That was the reason for the ground-zero search Angel and I were conducting.

"You remember when the Julius family vanished?" I asked. I picked up Susu's empty plate and my own and carried them over to the sink, admiring my new stoneware as I did every time I looked at it. Earth tones in a southwestern pattern . . . why on earth I, a native Georgian, felt compelled to have southwestern dishes I do not know.

"Yes," Susu said. "I'd just had Little Jimmy. You were working at the library, I think you'd only been there a year, right?"

"Right. Over six years ago, now." We shook our heads simultaneously at Time's inexorable march.

Susu looked at her watch and gave a little shriek. "Woops! Roe! I was supposed to pick up old Mrs. Newman at the beauty parlor ten minutes ago! I'm sorry, I've got to run! I invited myself and then I stick you with the dishes," she wailed, and yanked her car keys out of her purse on her way out the front door.

I stuck the dishes unceremoniously in the dishwasher, started our supper pork chops marinating in honey and soy sauce and garlic, and sat down to make one of those lists that were supposed to make me much more efficient.

1. Finish measuring the house.

2. Talk to Miss Neecy about Essie Nyland, also the Zinsners—where was the boarded-up closet?

3. Possible to find the boyfriend, Harley Dimmoch?

4. See if Parnell Engle will tell me about the day he poured the concrete.

5. Ask Lynn or Arthur if I could see the file on the Julius disappearance, or if he would just tell me about it in detail.

6. See if I could worm anything out of Mrs. Totino's lawyer, Bubba Sewell (who was incidentally my lawyer and the husband of my friend, the former Lizanne Buckley).

I was pleased. This looked as if it would keep me busy for quite a while. Right now, busy-ness was what

I wanted. Maybe while I worked on the problem of the Juliuses, the problem of my husband's secret life would sort of solve itself.

Right.

CHAIR A NO A NON
he and Meanwhile I wore ro the princes of las
Aprox the problem of my Lada d before the
world and of some to
Ruge

TEN

"SALLY," I SAID QUIETLY into the telephone on Martin's desk. "I want to have lunch with you at my place or your place soon, okay? I need to ask you some questions. You covered the Julius disappearance, didn't you? Do you still have a file on it somewhere, of your notes you took at the time?" Sally, cohostess at my bridal shower, had worked at the *Lawrenceton Sentinel* for at least fifteen years.

"I don't keep my notes on fiftieth wedding anniversaries or who won the watermelon-seed-spitting contest, but I do keep my notes on major crimes."

She sounded a little testy.

"Okay, okay!" I said hastily. "I'm sorry. I don't know how reporters do things!"

"Yes, I have the file right here," she said in a mollified tone. "And I can certainly understand why you're interested. My better half—well, my other half—is attending a seminar in Augusta on interrogation techniques, so I'm footloose and fancy free for two days. What suits you?"

"What about here, tomorrow, for lunch at noon?" I asked. I knew Sally, like all of Lawrenceton, wanted to see the house.

I hung up as Martin came down the stairs, sweating and relaxed after his session with the Soloflex. He played racquetball at the Athletic Club, too, but sometimes the hours didn't suit him. He liked having the exercise equipment at home.

"I'm sweaty," he warned me. I didn't care since I could use a shower myself after my work in the garage that morning. Angel and I had finished our measurements later in the afternoon, and there was a four-inch question mark running down the middle of the garage, but I figured that was just where Mrs. Zinsner had demanded Mr. Zinsner make it a two-car garage. I didn't think four inches was enough space to hide three bodies, and Angel agreed.

I hugged Martin, sliding my hands around his waist and up his back.

"Roe," he said hesitantly.

"Um?"

"Are you mad?"

"Yes. But I'm working on it."

"Working on it."

"Yeah. I suppose you didn't tell me all that before we got married in case I wouldn't marry you if I knew it. Is that right? Or did you just hope I wouldn't ever ask? Or did you just think I was desperate or stupid enough not to notice that there were a few holes in your story?"

"Well . . ."

"I'll give you a clue, Martin. There's only one correct answer to that."

"I was afraid you wouldn't marry me if you knew."

"And that was the correct answer."

"Good."

"So now I have to decide how I feel about you wanting me to enter into marriage, a very serious thing, not knowing all the facts about your life. Am I flattered that you were so anxious to keep me that you wouldn't risk it? Sure." I traced his spine with my fingernail and felt him shiver. "Am I angry that you treated me like some fifties little woman, the less I knew the better? You bet." I dug the fingernail in. He gasped. "Martin, you have to be honest with me. My self-respect—I can't stand being lied to, no matter how much I love you."

THE NEXT DAY, the day I was going to have Sally Allison over to lunch, Martin and I had also been invited to dinner at the home of one of Pan-Am Agra's division chiefs. This man, Bill Anderson, was a new employee, hired by Martin's boss and sent to Lawrenceton to evaluate and expand the plant's safety program. So I woke with a certain sense of anticipation. Martin was shaving as I groped past him into the bathroom for a quick stop on my way downstairs to the coffeepot. We were beginning to find our routine.

He liked to be at his desk when the other Pan-Am Agra executives arrived. And Martin always looked spic and span. His clothes were all expensive and he liked his shirts taken to the laundry to be starched, which frankly suited me. I didn't mind in the least dropping them by or picking them up. I hated ironing worse than anything in the world, and Martin, who could do a competent job of it, didn't have the time or inclination unless there was an emergency.

Luckily, we both liked noncommunication until coffee had been consumed. He would come downstairs and make his own breakfast and pour his own coffee. By that time I would have finished the front section of the paper, which I had fetched from the end of the driveway. He would read that, then I would hand him the inside sections. Martin was not much interested in team sports, I had noted silently. One-on-one sports, now that was something he checked the scores on.

When Martin had finished the paper and his breakfast, we had a brief conversation about appointments for the day. He went upstairs to brush his teeth. I poured another cup of coffee and worked the crossword puzzle in the newspaper.

He came downstairs, gathered his briefcase, checked with me to make sure we didn't need to talk about anything else, told me he was going to be out of his office most of the afternoon, and kissed me goodbye. He was gone by seven-thirty, or earlier.

I felt we had made a success of mornings, anyway. So far.

THIS MORNING Angel reported about eight-thirty.

"Shelby says," she began without preamble, "that

we need to find out if an aerial search was made, particularly of the fields around the house.''

"Hmm," I said, and made a note on my list. "I'll remember to ask that at lunch. A local reporter is a friend of mine, and she's coming over for lunch."

"You sure have a social life."

"Oh?"

"You're always having people over, or you go out, or people call you, seems like."

"I grew up here. I expect if you were still in the town you were born in, it would be the same."

"Maybe," said Angel doubtfully. "I've never had that many friends. When I grew up, we lived way out in the swamps. I had my brothers and sisters. What about you?"

"I have a half-brother, but he's in California. He's a lot younger than me."

"Well, except for some Cubans, it was just us out there. We pretty much kept to ourselves. When I was a teenager, I began to date...but even then, I was usually glad to get home. I wasn't much good at small talk, and if you didn't talk and drink, they wanted to do the other thing, and I didn't."

We smiled at each other for the first time.

Then Angel clammed up, and I realized she would only speak about herself in rationed drips, and I had had my allotment for the day.

We went out into the bright spring air to measure the outside of the house. Then we measured each inside room and drew a detailed map of our house.

"I guess sometime having this will come in handy," I sighed, a comparison of figures having shown that the walls were only walls and not secret compartments with grisly contents. So much for a hidden closet.

"Oh, I'm sure," Angel said drily. "The next time someone wants to know how to get to the bathroom, all you have to do is tell him to go forty-one inches from the newel post, due east, then north two feet."

I stared at her blankly for a second and then suddenly began to laugh.

Maybe our strange association was going to be more fun than either of us had anticipated.

Angel looked down at the plans.

"There's something in the attic," she said.

"What! What?"

"Nothing, most likely. But you know the chimney comes up from the living room, runs up one end of your bedroom where you have a fireplace, goes through the attic and out the roof."

"Right."

"It seemed to me that in the attic there was too much chimney."

"They might be sealed up in there," I said breathlessly.

"They might not. But we can see."

"Who can we call to knock it down?"

"Shoot, I can do it. But you got to think, here, Roe. What if there's nothing there? What if you're just knocking down a perfectly good chimney for the hell of it?"

"It's my chimney." I crossed my arms on my chest and looked up at her.

"So it is," she said. "Then let's go. You go up there and look, and I'll go to the garage and get a sledge-hammer and one or two other things we might need."

I let down the attic steps and climbed up. In the heat of the little attic, with sunlight coming in through the circular vent at the back of the house, I calmed down. The attic was floored, with the old original floorboards, wide and heavy. They creaked a little as I crossed to look at the chimney. Sure enough, the bricks looked a little different from the bricks downstairs, though I couldn't say they looked newer. And the chimney was wider.

I remained skeptical. I felt sure the police would have noticed fresh brickwork.

Angel came up the stairs in a moment, the sledge-hammer in her hand.

She eyed the bricks. She slid on a pair of clear plastic safety goggles. I stared at her.

"Brick fragments," she said practically. "You should stand well back, since you don't have safety glasses."

I retreated as far as I could, back into an area where I could barely stand, and on Angel's further advice I turned my back to the action. I heard the thunk as the hammer hit the bricks, and then more and more thunks, until gradually that sound became accompanied by the noises of cracking and falling.

Then Angel was still, and I turned.

She was looking at something in the heap of dislodged bricks and mortar chips.

"Oh, shit," she breathed.

I felt my skin crawl.

I scuttled over to Angel and stood by her looking down as she was doing.

In the rubble was a small figure wrapped in blankets blanketed by smoke and soot.

My hand went up over my mouth.

We stood for the longest moments of my life, staring down at that little bundle.

Then I knelt and with shaking hands began to unwrap the blanket. A tiny white face looked up at me.

I screamed bloody murder.

I think Angel did, too, though she afterward denied it hotly.

"It's a doll," she said, kneeling beside me and gripping my shoulders. "It's a doll, Roe. It's china." She shook me, and I believe she thought she was being gentle.

LATER ON, after we'd both showered and Angel had called a mason to come repair the chimney, we speculated on how the compartment had gotten sealed up, how the doll had been left inside. I figured that the story of Sarah May Zinsner's desire for a closet and her husband's sealing one up out of sheer cussedness had its basis in whatever had happened by the chimney. We ended up deciding that she'd ordered an extra frame of brickwork for shelving, to store—who knew what? Maybe she'd intended the shelving for the use of the maid who may have been living in the attic. But that final change had been the straw that had metaphorically broken John L. Zinsner's back. He'd had the shelves bricked up, and while the mason was working, perhaps one of the daughters of the house had set her wrapped-up "baby" temporarily (she thought) on the shelves. Now I had it, all these years later, and it had scared the hell out of Angel and me.

SOMEHOW, when my mother called while I was slicing strawberries for lunch, I didn't tell her about my morning's adventure. She would be horrified that I was looking for the Julius family; also, I didn't care to relate how deeply upset I'd been when I'd seen that tiny white face.

For once, she didn't sense that I was less than happy. That was remarkable, since we spoke on the phone or in person almost every day. She was all the family I had, since my father had moved with my stepbrother to California. That was something I had in common, I realized, with the Julius family. They had been nearly as untangled from the southern cobweb of family connections as I was.

"I had a closing this morning," Mother said. She was as proud of each sale as though it were her first, which I found sort of endearing. When I was in my early teens, when she'd begun to work but before she was independent and very successful, I'd felt each house she sold should be celebrated by a party. Mother seemed just as driven now as she had been after she'd separated from my father and become a needy wage earner; my father had never been too good about sending child support payments.

"Which one?" I asked, to show polite interest.

"The Anderson house," she said. "Remember, I told you I had it sold last week. I was scared until the last minute that they were going to back out. Some idiot told them about Tonia Lee Greenhouse." Tonia Lee, a local realtor, had been murdered in the master bedroom. "But it went through."

"That'll make Mandy happy. By the way," the similar names had reminded me, "we're going to dinner at Bill Anderson's tonight. You sold them a house, didn't you? What's his wife like?"

"Nice enough, not too bright, if I remember correctly. They're renting, with an option to buy."

After we said our good-byes, and I returned to my task at the sink, hurrying because the attic escapade had made me late, I tried to imagine what my mother would do in my present predicament—but it was like trying to picture the pope tap dancing.

SALLY ARRIVED punctually, in a very expensive outfit that she intended to wear to rags. Sally had been forty-two for a number of years. She was an attractive woman with short permed bronzey hair. She was neither slim nor fat, neither short nor tall.

During the past two or three years, Sally had been close to breaking into the big time with a larger paper, but it just hadn't happened. She had settled for being the mentor and terror of the young cub reporters who regularly came and went at the *Sentinel* as they learned their trade.

For the first time, Sally gave me a ritual hug. It was a recognition of the big things I'd undergone since last we met, the fact that I was now a respectable married woman, and not only married, but married to a real prize, an attractive plant manager who presumably had an excellent income. This really can all be conveyed in a hug.

"You look great, Roe," Sally pronounced.

I don't know why people seem impelled to tell brides that. Is regular sex supposed to make you prettier? A number of acquaintances had told me how great I looked since we'd come back from the honeymoon. Maybe only married sex made you look better.

"Thanks, Sally. Come on in and see the house."

"I haven't been in here for years. Not since it happened. Oh, who would have known there were hardwood floors! It looks wonderful!" Sally followed me around, exclaiming appropriately at each point of interest.

As I put lunch on the table, she told me all about her son Perry and the wonderful girl he'd met in his ther-

apy group, and about her husband Paul and the shak-
iness of their new marriage.

"Surely you can work it out, Sally! You had such
high hopes when you married him, and it's only been
a few months!"

"Fourteen," she said precisely, spearing a straw-
berry with her fork.

"Oh. Well. Would marriage counseling help, do you
think? Aubrey Scott is really good."

"Maybe," she said. "We'll talk about it when Paul
gets back from Augusta."

"So, can you tell me all about the disappearance?"
I asked gently, when she'd poked at her dill pickle for
a few seconds of recovery.

"Do you have the stories from the *Sentinel?*"

"Yes, the main one. I really want to know what you
didn't put in the paper, or what stuck out in your
mind. Were you out here then?"

"Along with a slew of other reporters. Though I did
get an exclusive for one day. The disappearance was
really hot for a while, until a week had passed with no
news. But being the local reporter paid off."

Sally laid down her fork and opened her briefcase.
She extracted a few pages of computer printout from
a file folder.

"Those are your notes?" I'd expected a spiral
notebook with scribbles.

"Yes," Sally said with a hint of surprise. "Of
course I put them on a disk when I get back to the office. Let me see . . . this will be a reconstruction." She

glanced over the pages, organizing herself, and nodded.

"When the police got here," she began . . .

*There's a old woman standing out in the drive-
way. She's small, and gray, and alternately distraught and grumpy. Her name, she says, is
Melba Totino, and she is the mother of Mrs. Julius, Hope Julius. They're all gone, she says:
Hope, and her husband T.C., and their girl,
Charity. They vanished in the night. She herself
had risen at her usual hour and gone over to the
house to prepare breakfast, as she always did. She
had expected all of them to be there, even Charity, who had been home sick the day before.
Charity is a sophomore at Lawrenceton High,
newly enrolled. She'd had a hard six weeks getting used to being in a new school, missing her
boyfriend, but finally she'd adjusted. She'd had
a low fever the past couple of days. But Charity,
sick or not, now wasn't in the house.*

*Melba Totino goes in by the front door, since
the back door of the kitchen faced outward over
a new expanse of concrete, poured the day before to make a patio. She is unsure whether or not
it's okay to walk on the concrete yet, so she goes
to the front. The door's unlocked. No lights on
inside. No stirring, no movement.*

Mrs. Totino steps inside hesitantly, calling. She doesn't want to stroll in without warning. But no one answers her call. She creeps through the house, now anxious, looking about for signs of the untoward. The house is clean and peaceful. The cuckoo clock in the living room makes its brainless noise, and the old lady jumps.

Where is her daughter? Where is Hope? With approaching panic, the old lady finally screams up the stairs, but no one answers. Telling herself she is being ridiculous, and she'll give them a real talking-to when they come home, Melba Totino sits at the kitchen table, waiting for someone to come. She doesn't dare to touch a thing. The dishes are all put away. There is no coffee perking, nothing baking in the oven. After half an hour, she walks back out the front door and looks in the garage. She hadn't bothered on her way over—why would she?

And now, as far as she can see, everything is the same. She doesn't drive, she doesn't know anything about cars, but this car is her daughter's family car, the truck is her son-in-law's pickup, with "Julius Home Carpentry" proudly painted on the side, phone number right below. No one is in either vehicle.

She goes from the entrance to the garage past the stairs leading up to her apartment, across the covered walkway over to the house, into the big backyard. She is glad she has her sweater on, there's a nip in the air for sure. There's a turkey buzzard circling in the sky. The yard itself is empty. She looks up to the second story of the house, hoping to see movement at Charity's window, but there is nothing.

Bewildered, trying to keep her terror a secret from herself, the old woman walks slowly back to the front of the house, still trying to keep pristine that new concrete that the owners of the house will never see again. Finally, after some interminable hours, she calls the police.

"Parnell Engle drove by that morning in his pickup truck," Sally explained, "and since he'd poured the concrete the day before, naturally he glanced at the place as he went by. After he saw all the police cars there, he just happened to stop by the paper to check on his classified ad, and just happened to wander into the newsroom and let me know what he'd seen."

"Naturally," I agreed.

"Of course, this was a couple of years before he 'found the Lord,'" Sally said. "Lucky for me, because I was able to talk to the old lady before any other reporters even knew something had happened. By the next day she wasn't talking to anyone. Wonder where she is now?"

"In Peachtree Leisure Apartments," I said smugly. "She gave me a wedding present." It was not often I got to impart news to Sally.

"It's odd she chose to stay here, with no family. I gather she and her sister had been living in New Orleans. Wonder why she didn't go back?"

"She told me she was waiting for the Juliuses to turn up."

Sally shuddered, and took a sip of her iced tea. "That's creepy in more ways than one. You know, Hope Julius would be dead by now, even if she was alive."

I raised my eyebrows, and after a second, Sally realized what she'd said. She shook her head in self-exasperation.

"What I mean is, Hope Julius had cancer," Sally explained. "She had ovarian cancer, I think, very advanced. Though there was apparently little hope, she was undergoing radiation treatment in Atlanta. All her hair had fallen out... I remember seeing one wig and one empty stand in her room when the police let me walk through the house... Mrs. Totino said it was okay. One wig, a curly one that she wore almost every day, was gone. The one that was left was fancier, like she'd had her hair put up. She wore that one to church and parties."

"Oooo," I said. "That's *awful*." A woman's false hair, sitting there in her room when the woman was gone.

"It really was," Sally agreed. She turned a page in her notebook.

"Why was the wig there, I wonder? That makes it look bad for Mrs. Julius."

"Yes, it does. She wouldn't leave without her extra wig, would she? And the wig made the whole scene eerier . . . like Martians had beamed them up right after they'd made their beds that morning, but before they'd gone down to breakfast."

"They'd made their beds," I repeated.

"Yes, unless something happened during the night, before they went to bed but after Mrs. Totino had gone to sleep up in her apartment."

"And what time was that, do you remember?"

"Yes, I have it here . . . nine-thirty, she said. She was extra tired from all the activity of the day . . . the Dimmoch boy coming to visit Charity and help T.C., Parnell coming to pour the patio."

It was hard picturing that as exhausting since someone else had done all the work. I said as much to Sally.

"Yes, but you see, since her daughter was so ill she'd been doing most of the cooking, the evening meals anyway, and lots of the laundry, I gathered."

"Maybe that was why T.C. was agreeable to building her the apartment? Because Hope was so sick?"

"That's what I presumed. I never met him. The few people who did meet him, like Parnell Engle, liked him, and liked Hope, too. The picture I get is of a rigid kind of man, very honest and aboveboard, very meticulous in his dealings, punctual, orderly; of course, some of that might be from being in the service for so long. As far as I can tell, Hope was not a strong person, emotionally or physically, and I'm sure her illness had sapped her."

"And Charity?"

"Charity was a typical teenager, according to the local kids who knew her for a few weeks. She talked all the time about her boyfriend she'd had to leave behind when she moved here, but most of the girls I interviewed seemed to feel that was a ploy to make her look important. Though since the Dimmoch boy cared enough to drive over, I guess they were wrong. Her grades, if I am remembering correctly, weren't that good, implying either that she wasn't bright or that she was more interested in other things; don't know which. She was an attractive girl, they all said that in one way or another, even though she didn't seem so pretty in a photo. I managed to talk to a couple of kids who knew her when she lived in Columbia, and they all spoke of her as being a strong girl, one with a lot of adult qualities, especially after her mother got sick."

I offered Sally another glass of tea. She looked down at her wrist.

"No, thanks. I've got to be at a City Council meeting in ten minutes."

Sally left me with a lot to think about as I put the dishes in the dishwasher. And I realized I'd forgotten to ask her about the aerial search.

After I saw Angel leave on some errand of her own that afternoon, I did something peculiar.

I retraced Mrs. Totino's movements of the morning of the disappearance—no, the morning the disappearance was reported—as she had told them to Sally. I walked in the front door, looked around, went to the kitchen, went out the front door again, looked in the garage, went between the garage and the house to the backyard. I looked around it, and up at the window of our guest bedroom, the room that had been Charity's. Then I went in the front door yet another time.

I was certainly glad we lived out in the country so no one would see this bizarre exercise, which netted me exactly nothing but chills up and down my spine.

I CALLED Lynn Liggett Smith that afternoon. Conversations between Lynn and me were always egg-walking exercises. On the one hand, she'd married Arthur Smith, the policeman whom I'd dated and been very fond of for months before he up and married Lynn—who was pregnant. I didn't care so much about that anymore, but Lynn felt a certain delicacy. On the other hand, we would have liked each other if it hadn't been for that, I'd always thought.

"How's Lorna?" I asked. I pictured Lynn at her desk at the Lawrenceton police station, tall, slim Lynn who'd lost all her baby-weight very fast and resumed her tailored suits and bright blouses with ease. I'd seen Lynn at the wedding, but of course she and Arthur hadn't brought the baby. Since I'd seen Lorna being born, I was always interested in her progress. "Is she walking yet?" I had a very shaky idea of baby chronology.

"She's been walking for months now," Lynn said. "And she's talking. She knows at least forty words!"

"Eating real food?"

"Oh, yes! You ought to see Arthur feeding her yogurt."

I thought I would pass that up.

"So what can I help you with today, Roe?"

"I wondered," I said, "if you would mind very much looking in the file on the Julius disappearance, and telling me exactly how the police searched."

Long silence.

"That's all you want to know?" Lynn asked cautiously.

"Yes, I think so."

"I can't think of a good reason why not."

The phone clunked as it hit Lynn's desk, and I heard other detectives talking in the background as the click of Lynn's pumps receded.

With the phone clamped awkwardly between my shoulder and ear, I wiped the kitchen counter. I tried to decide what I'd wear to dinner that night. Should we take a bottle of wine with us? What if the Andersons were teetotal? Lots of people in this area were.

"Roe?"

I jumped. The telephone was speaking to me.

"Every inch of the house was searched, and the garage apartment, too. No bloodstains. No signs of foul play. Gas in both vehicles, both vehicles running normally...so they hadn't been disabled. Beds stripped and mattresses tested...yard gone over inch by inch. The fields visually surveyed. According to the file, Jack Burns requested an aerial search but the city didn't have enough money left in the budget to pay for one."

"Golly. Since there wasn't enough money, one wasn't done?"

"You got it."

"That's wrong."

"That's fiscal responsibility."

"I just never thought about police department budgets not permitting things like that."

Lynn laughed sardonically, and did a good job of it, too. "Budgets don't permit lots of things we'd like to do. Our budget doesn't even permit us to do some of the things we need, much less the things we'd like."

"Oh," I said inadequately, still at a loss.

"But short of that, the investigation was very thorough. And the search was meticulous. There was a complete search of the house, an exhaustive search of the yard and the field around the house, and a lab examination of the two vehicles, all of which turned up absolutely nothing. Bus stations, airlines, train stations, all queried for anyone answering the description of any or all members of the family. That took some time, since they were all more or less average looking, though Hope was visibly ill. But no leads.''

"Eerie." I jumped at the sound of the pet door as Madeleine entered. She walked over to her food bowl and deposited something in it, something furry and dead.

"Jack still talks about that case, when he's had a beer or two. Which is more often—" Lynn stopped, reconsidered, and changed the subject. "So how's your husband?"

"He's fine," I said, a little surprised. Arthur had strong views about Martin, and he had shared them with Lynn, I could tell.

"He is a little older than you?"

"Fifteen years. Well, fourteen plus."

I could feel my brows contracting over my nose. I took off my glasses—the tortoiseshell pair today—and rubbed the little spot where tension always gathered. Madeleine was waiting for me to come over and compliment her.

"I want to talk to you sometime soon," Lynn said, with an air of suddenly made decision.

Arthur and Lynn, through some law-enforcement channel, had heard something about Martin's former activities, I thought. All I needed at this point was someone else lecturing me. Or telling me something I didn't know about my own husband, pitying me.

"I'll give you a call when I'm free," I said.

ELEVEN

A SPRING DINNER at an employee's house; our first social engagement as a couple since our wedding. I finally chose a short-sleeved bright cotton dress and pumps. Martin brushed my hair for me, something he enjoyed doing. I was ready to get it cut. Its waviness and resultant bushiness made it a pain if it got too long, but Martin really liked it below my shoulders. I would tolerate the extra trouble until another Georgia summer. Since the dress was blue and red, I wore my red glasses, and I felt they added a cheerful touch. For some reason, my husband found them amusing.

Martin wore a suit, but when we got to the Andersons', only a few houses down Plantation Drive from my mother's, we found Bill Anderson shedding his tie.

"It's already heating up for summer," he said, "let's get rid of these things. The ladies won't mind, will you, Roe? Bettina?"

Bettina Anderson, a copper-haired, heavy woman in her mid-forties, murmured, "Of course not!" at exactly the same moment I did.

Our host took Martin down the hall to deposit his coat. They were gone a little longer than such an errand warranted. While they were gone, I asked Bettina if there was anything I could help her with, and since she didn't know me, she had to say there was nothing.

I was glad we hadn't brought the wine when we were offered nothing to drink stronger than iced tea.

Bill and Martin reappeared, Martin wearing a scowl that he made an effort to smooth out. Bettina vanished into the kitchen within a few minutes and was obviously flustered, but I noticed that when the doorbell rang again, it was Bettina who answered it.

I wondered how long the Andersons had been married. They didn't actually talk to each other very much.

To my pleasure, the other dinner guests were Bubba Sewell and his wife, my friend Lizanne Sewell, nee Buckley. Bubba is an up-and-coming lawyer and legislator, and Lizanne is beautiful and full-bodied, with a voice as slow and warm as butter melting on corn. They had married a few months before we had, and the supper they'd given us had been the best party we'd had as an engaged couple.

I gave Lizanne a half-hug, rather than a full frontal hug, befitting our friendship and the length of time we hadn't seen each other.

Bettina turned down Lizanne's offer to help as well; so she was certainly determined to keep us "company." We chattered away while our hostess slaved out of sight in the kitchen and dining room. Lizanne inquired about the honeymoon, but without envy: She never wanted to leave the United States, she said.

"You don't know where you are in those other countries," she said darkly. "Anything can happen."

I could see Bill Anderson had overheard this and was about to take issue, an incredulous look on his face. (I was beginning not to like Bill, and unless I was mistaken, Martin didn't like him either. I wondered if this was something we would have to do often, dine with people with whom we had nothing in common.)

"Are you enjoying not having to go to work every morning?" I asked Lizanne instantly, to spare her discomfort. (Lizanne probably wouldn't care one bit what Bill Anderson or anyone else thought about her opinions, but her husband would.)

"Oh...it's all right," Lizanne said thoughtfully. "There's a lot to do on the house, yet. I'm on some good-works committees...that was Bubba's idea." She seemed slightly amused at Bubba's efforts to get her into his own up-and-coming pattern.

We were called to the dining room at that moment, and since I had my own agenda, I was pleased to see I was seated between Martin and Bubba at the round table.

After the flurry of passing and serving and complimenting an anxious Bettina on the chicken and rice and broccoli and salad, I quietly asked our state representative if he had been the lawyer in charge of the Julius estate since their disappearance. It was heartless of me, since the conversation had turned to regional football.

"Yes," he said, dabbing his mustache carefully with his napkin. "I handled the house purchase, when Mrs. Zinsner sold the house to T.C. Julius. So after they vanished, Mrs. Totino asked me to continue as the lawyer in the case."

"What's the law about disappearances, Bubba?"

"According to Georgia law, missing people can be declared dead after seven years," Bubba told me. "But Mrs. Totino was able to show she was the sole remaining relative of the family, and since she had very little without their support—she'd been living with a sister in New Orleans, scraping by with Social Security—we went to court and got her appointed conservator of the estate, so I could arrange for her to have enough money to live on. After a year, we got a letter of administration, so she could sell the property whenever she could find a buyer. Of course, this is all a matter of public record," he concluded cautiously.

"So in a few months, the Juliuses will be declared dead."

"Yes, then the remainder of their estate will be Mrs. Totino's."

"The house sale money."

"Oh, no. Not just the house sale money. He'd been saving for a while, to start his own business when he retired from the Army." And Bubba indicated by the set of his mouth that this was the end of the conversation about the Julius family's financial resources.

"Did you like him?" I asked, after we'd eaten quietly for a minute.

"He was a rough man," Bubba said thoughtfully. "Very much...'everything goes as I say in my family.' But he wasn't mean."

"Did you meet the others?"

"Oh, yes. I met Mrs. Julius when they bought the house. Very sick, very glad to be within driving distance of all the hospitals in Atlanta. A quiet woman. The daughter was just a teenager; not giggly. That's all I remember about her."

Then our host asked Bubba what was coming up in the legislature that we needed to know about, and my conversation with him about the Julius family was over.

On the way home, I related all this to Martin, who listened abstractedly. That wasn't like Martin, who was willing to be interested in the Julius disappearance if I was.

"I have to fly to Guatemala next week," he told me.

"Oh, Martin! I thought you weren't going to have to travel as much now that you're not based in Chicago."

"I thought so, too, Roe."

He was so curt that I glanced over with some surprise. Martin was visibly worried.

"How long will you be gone?"

"Oh, I don't know. As long as it takes...maybe three days."

"Could...maybe I could go, too?"

"Wait till we get home; I can't pay attention to this conversation while I'm driving."

I bit my lip in mortification. When we got home, I stalked straight into the house.

He was just getting out of the car to open my door, and I caught him off guard. He didn't catch up to me until I was halfway down the sidewalk to the kitchen side door.

Then he put his hand on my shoulder and began, "Roe, what I meant..."

I shook his hand off. "Don't you talk to me," I said, keeping my voice low because of the Youngbloods. Here we lived a mile out of town, and I still couldn't scream at my husband in my own yard. "Don't you say *one word.*"

I stomped up the stairs, shut the door to our bedroom, and sat on the bed.

What was the matter with me? I'd never had open quarrels with anyone in my life, and here I was brawling with my husband, and I'd been within an ace of hitting him, something I'd also never done. This was so *trashy.*

I had to do some thinking, and now. Our relationship had always been more emotional than any I'd ever had, more volatile. But these bright, hot feelings had always served to leap the chasms between us, I realized, sitting on the end of our new bedspread in our new house with my new wedding ring on my finger. I took off my shoes and sat on the floor. Somehow I could think better.

"He's still not telling me the truth," I said out loud, and knew that was it.

I could hear him faintly, stomping about downstairs. Fixing himself a drink, I decided. I felt only stunned wonder—how had I ended up sitting on the floor in my bedroom, angry and grieved, in love with a man who lived a life in secret? I remembered Cindy Bartell saying, "He won't cheat on you. But he won't ever tell you everything, either."

I had a moment of sheer rage and self-pity, during which I asked myself all those senseless questions. What had I done to deserve this? Now that I'd finally, finally gotten married, why wasn't it all roses? If he loved me, why didn't he treat me perfectly?

I lay back on the floor, looking up at the ceiling. More important, what was I going to do during the next hour?

A creaking announced Martin's progress up the stairs and across the landing.

"I won't knock at my own bedroom door," he said, from outside.

I stared at the ceiling even harder.

The door opened slowly. Perhaps he was afraid I'd throw something at him? An intriguing mental image. Maybe Cindy had thrown things.

He appeared at my feet, two icy glasses of what appeared to be 7-and-7 in his hands. I saw the wet stain on his off-white shirt, where he'd tucked the extra glass between arm and chest while he'd used his other hand to open the door.

"What are you doing, Roe?"

"Thinking."

"Are you going to talk to me?"

"Are you going to talk to *me?*"

He sat on the stool in front of my vanity table. He leaned over to hand me a drink. I held it centered under my breasts with both hands gripping the heavy glass.

"I still..." he began. He stopped, looked around as if a reprieve would come, took a drink. I looked up at him from the floor, waiting.

"I still sell guns."

I felt as if the ceiling had fallen on my head.

"Do you want to know any more about it than that?"

"No," I said. "Not now."

"I don't think Bill Anderson is who he says he is," Martin said.

I cut my gaze over to him without turning my head.

"I think he's government."

I looked back at my glass. "I thought you were government."

His mouth went down at one corner.

"I thought I was, too. I suspect something's changed that I don't know about. That's why I need to go to Guatemala. Something's come unglued."

I struggled with so many questions I couldn't decide what to ask first. Did I really want to know the answers to any of them?

"Are you really a man with a regular job with a real company?" I asked, hating the way my voice faltered.

He looked sad. "I'm everything I ever told you I was. Just—other things, too."

"Then why couldn't you be satisfied?" I said bitterly and futilely.

I sat up, tears coursing down my cheeks without my knowing they had started, not sobbing, just—watering my dress. I took a drink from my glass; yes, it was 7-and-7.

When I could bear to, I looked at him.

"Will you stay?" he asked.

We looked at each other for a long moment.

"Yes," I said. "For a while."

I NEVER FINISHED that drink, yet the next morning I felt I had a hangover. I had to take my mind off my life. I dressed briskly, putting on powdered blush more heavily than usual because I looked like hell warmed over, and went to Parnell Engle's cement business.

It was a small operation north of Lawrenceton. There were heaps of different kinds of gravel and sand dotting the fenced-in area, and a couple of large cement trucks were rumbling around doing whatever they had to do. The office was barren and utilitarian to a degree I hadn't seen in years. There was a cracked leather couch, a few black file cabinets, and a desk in the outer office. That desk was commanded by a squat woman in stretch pants and an incongruous gauzy blouse that was intended to camouflage rolls of fat. She had good-humored eyes peering out of a round face, and she was dealing with someone over the phone in a a very firm way.

"If we told you it would be there by noon, it will be there by noon. Mr. Engle don't promise nothing he can't do. Now the rain, we cain't control the rain... No, they cain't come sooner, all our trucks are tied up till then... I know the weather said rain, but like I told you... All right then, we'll see you *at noon*." And she hung up with a certain force. There was an old Underwood typewriter on the desk, and not a computer in sight.

"Is Mr. Engle in?" I asked.

"Parnell!" she yelled toward the door behind her. "Someone here to see you."

Parnell appeared in the door in a moment dressed in blue jeans, work boots, and a khaki shirt, his hand full of papers.

"Oh," he said unenthusiastically. "Roe Teagarden. You enjoying all that money my cousin left you?"

"Yes," I said baldly.

After a moment of Dodge-City staring at each other, Parnell cracked a smile. "Well, at least the Lord has shined on you," he said. "I hear you got married last month. God meant for woman to be a companion to man."

"Amen," I said sadly.

"You need to talk to me?"

"Yes, if you have a minute."

"That's about all I do have, but come on in." He made a nearly gracious sweep with his handful of papers, and I went across the creaking wooden floor to Parnell's sanctum. I felt a surge of fondness for Parnell; his office was exactly what I expected. It was as dilapidated as the outer room, and there was a large reproduction of the Last Supper on the wall, and plaques with Bible verses were stuck here and there, along with a huge map of the country and a calendar that featured scenery rather than women.

"You know I bought the Julius house," I said directly. Parnell neither expected nor appreciated small talk. "I want to know about the day you poured the patio there."

"I went over and over it at the time," he remarked. "And I don't know why you want to know, but I suppose it's none of my business. It's been a long time since I thought of that day."

He leaned back in his chair, wove his fingers together across his lean stomach. He pursed his thin lips for a moment, then began. "I was still working most of the jobs I got myself. I've prospered in the last few years, praise the Lord. But when T.C. called, I was glad to come. He'd made the form himself, it was all ready, he told me. I knew he was trying to set up his own carpentry business, handyman work, that kind of thing, so I knew he'd have done a competent job. So I went out there with the truck and the black man working for me then, Washington Prescott, he's dead now, had an aneurysm. We got there. The form looked fine, just like I expected. There was some rubble down in it, like people throw in sometimes, extra bricks, things you want to get rid of; but nothing like a body or anything that could have held a body. Stones, old bricks, seems like I remember a couple of pieces of cloth, rag. The girl Charity came out and said hi, I'd met the family before at church so I knew her. She said her dad had gone on an errand and called to say he wouldn't make it back in time, I should just go on and pour and send him a bill.''

"You never saw him?''

"Just said that, didn't I?''

"Did you see other members of the family?''

"I'm about to tell you. You're the one wanting to know all about it.''

"Sorry.''

"Charity's boyfriend, Harley, came out to help if I needed him. And the mother-in-law, don't remember her name, came out of the garage apartment and watched us for a spell. While we were pouring, Washington was in the form getting everything to flow right, and then we were both finishing it. I could see in the kitchen window. Hope was in there wearing an apron, fixing supper, looked like. She waved at me but didn't come out to speak. I thought, She must be in a hurry. They must be going out later.''

"She was usually friendly?''

"Hope? Oh, yes, she was a friendly woman, meek. That cancer was really draining her, but that day she looked better and moved easier than she had in the month or two I'd known her."

He'd seen every member of the Julius family but T.C.

"Was the light in the kitchen on?" I asked.

"No, I don't think so. There was still plenty of light. I got there at four, and it was late October; it wasn't real bright, come to think of it. But it was Hope I saw."

"And there's no way that after you left, bodies could have been put in the concrete."

"I went out late the next day after I'd talked to the police. That concrete was exactly like me and Washington left it, and no one had touched it."

Parnell said this with a finality that was absolutely believable. He leaned up in his chair to a squeal of springs, and said, "Now, I think that's it, Roe."

He got up to walk me to the door, so I slung my purse over my shoulder and obediently preceded him. I thought of one last question.

"Parnell, why did you think Mrs. Julius was going out later?"

"Well," he said, and then stopped dead. "Now why did I?" he wondered, scratching the side of his nose with the papers he'd picked up again. His narrow face went blank as he rummaged through his memory. "Because of the wig," he said, pleased at his ability to recall. "Hope was wearing her Sunday wig."

NEXT I WENT TO the church.

I couldn't think of anywhere else to go.

It was unlocked. I could see across the right angle formed by the church and the parish hall, where the office was. Aubrey was seated at his desk. But I went in the church. It was warm and dusty. I sat at the back, let down a kneeler, and slid down on it.

I was hoping to bring order to chaos.

I'd promised Martin to stay with him, when we married. I loved him.

But he was—a Bad Guy. Or, at the very least, a Not-So-Good Guy.

I winced as I formulated the thought, but I couldn't deny its truth.

If someone came to me—say, Aubrey—and told me, "I know a man who sells arms illegally to desperate people in Latin America," what would I assume?

I would assume that this man was bad, because no matter what else was good in his life, it would not balance that piece of—evil.

This man who was doing that evil act was my husband, the man who had made alternate honeymoon plans so he'd be sure I was happy, the man who thought he was extremely lucky to marry me, the man who'd fought a horrible war in Vietnam, a man who loved and supported an ungrateful son.

I was convinced Martin was doing what he was doing not because he was intrinsically evil but because he was addicted to danger, adventure, and maybe because he thought he was serving his country. But what he was doing would poison our life together, no matter how much good that life contained. He was my sweetheart, he was my lover, he was an agricultural company executive, he was a veteran, he was an athlete, but I could not forget what else he did.

I cried for a while. I heard the door of the church open quietly. I felt someone standing in the narthex behind me: Aubrey. He must have noticed my car. But I didn't turn around because I didn't want him to see my face. After a while I felt his hand brush my hair in a caress and rest lightly on my shoulder. He gave me a pat, and I heard the door squeak shut behind him.

PEACHTREE Leisure Apartments. A different security guard, also black, less formidable and less good-natured. This man's name was Roosevelt, which I was sure pleased Mrs. Totino. She was less pleased with me, however; her voice, which I could hear crackling over the lobby phone, was not enthusiastic. Perhaps she was regretting the purple and silver placemats.

"You been crying," she said sharply, standing back from her door with none too gracious an air. Why the sudden coolness? I remembered she had a reputation for being disagreeable. Maybe she'd just reverted to character.

"I wanted to ask you something," I said. "I'm sorry I didn't call before I came." Actually, that had been a stroke of luck, I now considered.

She wasn't going to ask me to sit.

"What?" she said rudely.

"The day the concrete was poured for the patio..."

She nodded curtly, her thin bent figure outlined in the sun coming through the one window in the cramped and crowded living room.

"Can you think of any reason why your daughter would be wearing her Sunday wig?"

"Go!" she shrieked at me suddenly. "Go! Go! Go! You bought the house! That's the end of it! You can't leave it alone, can you? We'll never know! You know what one old fool here told me? Told me they'd got eaten by Martians! I've listened to it for years. I just can't stand it!"

Utterly taken aback and deeply embarrassed at having provoked such a ruckus—doors were opening up and down the hall—I stepped back and gave her the room she needed to slam the door in my face.

To CAP OFF a perfect twenty-four hours, Martin telephoned from work to say his superior at the main office in Chicago had called an urgent meeting of all plant managers for as soon as everyone could get there. He'd come home to pack and I hadn't been there, and no one had known where I was.

Whom had he asked? I wondered.

"So I'll have to fly straight from Chicago to Guatemala," he said.

I made a little noise of protest. I couldn't reach any decision about my life with Martin, but I knew I would miss him and I hated for him to leave the country before we could resolve our problems.

"Roe," he said in a more private, less brisk, voice. "I'm going to quit."

Unfortunately, I started crying again.

"Promise," I sobbed, like a nine-year-old.

"I promise," he said. "This last trip is it. I'll start disentangling myself while I'm down there. There are people I have to talk to, arrangements I have to make. But it's over for me."

"Thank God," I said.

I thought I'd wept more in my four-week marriage to Martin than I had in the previous four years.

TWELVE

THE NEXT DAY, I called Harley Dimmoch's parents to find out where their son was now. The name was not exactly common, and Columbia, South Carolina, is not that big. There were three Dimmochs; the second listing was the right one.

I told Harley Dimmoch's mother that I had just bought the house the Julius family lived in. "I'm interested in the history of the house. I was hoping he could tell me about the day before they disappeared."

"He doesn't like to talk about it. He was really sweet on the girl, you know."

"Charity."

"Yes. I hadn't thought of that in a year or two, Harley is so different now."

"Does he live in Columbia with you?"

"No, he lives close to the Gulf Coast now, working in a lumber yard. He's got a girlfriend now, for several years he's been seeing this young woman. He comes home to visit about once a year, to let us have a look at him."

"And you say he doesn't talk about Charity's disappearance?"

"No, he's real touchy about it. His dad and me, we always thought he felt kind of guilty. Like if he'd stayed instead of coming on home that night, he could have stopped whatever happened.''

"So he came home the day—''

"He came home very late the night before Mrs. Totino found they were gone. Oh, the police came over here and talked to him forever, we were afraid he'd lose his temper, which he's a little prone to do, and say something that would make them think he'd done it..."

I liked this woman. She was loquacious.

"But he just seemed stunned, like. He hardly knew what he was doing. He told us a thousand times, 'Mama, Daddy, I helped Mr. Julius with the roof and I watched the man pour the concrete for the patio and I ate supper, and I left.' "

"He never mentioned they were quarreling with each other, or strangers came to the door, or anything odd?" I was trolling, now.

"No, everything was just as usual, he kept on telling me that like we doubted him. And the police went over and over that old car of his, like to drove us crazy. He was just nuts about Charity. He has never been the same since that time."

"Oh, really?"

"Yes, he just couldn't settle down after that. He is older than—well, Charity was fifteen or sixteen, and Harley was eighteen when it happened. It's hard to believe my baby is twenty-four now, almost twenty-five! We had hoped he'd stay with us, maybe think about going to a junior college, or something like that.

He had just gotten laid off at his first job when he went over to see Charity that time. But after it happened, he just wanted to take off on his own, didn't want to stay around here. And the shock of it. It's like he don't want more surprises, ever in his life again. He don't like phone calls if he's not expecting us to call. We call him on Sunday, or not at all. We don't drive down to see him on the spur of the moment, so to speak, we tell him way in advance.''

I made an indeterminate sound that was meant to be encouraging.

''So I'd better not give you his number, Miss. Because he wouldn't appreciate a phone call from out of the blue. But if you'll give me your number, I'll pass it on to him the next time we speak.''

I gave her my name and phone number, thanked her sincerely, and hung up.

I related this conversation to Angel as we sat on the front porch with lemonade two days later. The house was measured all over and we'd knocked on walls for hollow places. We'd scanned the yard. Neecy Dawson, whom I wanted to ask about the sealed-up closet, had gone to Natchez to tour antebellum homes with a busload of other ladies. Bettina Anderson had left a message on my answering machine. I'd seen my mother and John off to a real estate brokers' convention in Tucson, and the weather was swiftly getting hotter. There was never enough spring in Georgia.

Martin had called to say he'd arrived in Chicago, and Emily Kaye had called to ask me to join St.

James's Altar Guild. Both calls had made me anxious, though on different levels. Martin had sounded worried but determined; it was the worried part that frightened me. Would it be easy to extricate himself from this business? Emily, in her very nicest way, had quite refused to take no for an answer and had sweetly demanded I attend the Altar Guild meeting today to find out more about it.

"So what have you learned?" Angel was asking in her flat Florida voice.

"I have learned," I began slowly, "that Mrs. Julius was wearing her Sunday wig on a weekday night. I have learned that Mrs. Totino doesn't want to talk about the disappearance anymore. I have learned that there were no bodies under the concrete, and none could have been put there afterward. I have learned that Harley Dimmoch was a changed person after Charity Julius disappeared, but that at the time the police were satisfied with his story, because Mrs. Totino saw the Juliuses after he left—presumably."

"So Mrs. Totino's word is all you have that they were alive?"

"Yes," I conceded. "But after all, she's the mother of the woman who's missing. She was part of the family. Her daughter had cancer."

"Maybe we should talk to the sister. Mrs. Totino's sister. The one in Metaire."

"I don't know what she could tell me. According to Mrs. Totino, the sister's never been up here. Mrs. Totino is so in love with New Orleans she goes down there every now and then, she says, though somehow it sounded like the sister wasn't exactly happy to have her.''

"Wonder why?"

"Well, she can certainly pitch a fit when she wants to, and evidently from what the security guard said the first day I visited, she has a reputation for being unpleasant.''

"If she's such a bitch, how come the Juliuses wanted her around?''

"To help in the house, while Mrs. Julius was having her cancer treatments, I guess.''

"But wouldn't that have made everything worse? I mean, you've got a sick woman, and a teenage girl mad because she had to move away from her boyfriend, and a husband trying to start his own business in a new town. Wouldn't a woman like that be more trouble than she was worth? They could've hired a maid cheaper than building onto the garage.''

Put like that, it *was* mysterious. I would mull it over when I had the time. Right now I had to meet with the members of the Altar Guild, presumably to talk about altar topics, whatever that might include.

"I've got to go," I said reluctantly. I moved to pick up the glasses.

"I'll get them," Angel said. "I'll just put them in the kitchen and lock the door on my way out.''

So we went inside together, since I needed my purse and keys. I was wearing what I hoped was a suitable tailored khaki skirt and a striped blouse with a bright yellow barrette to hold back my hair, and my soberest pair of glasses, the ones with the tortoiseshell rims. My purse was right inside, at the front door, so I was going down the front porch steps before Angel had even reached the kitchen. It was warm, but not that breathless glaring heat you get in a full-blown Georgia summer. I scuffled through the grass, thinking that buying a riding mower at Sears might be a good idea; the yard was so big.

Madeleine suddenly ran from the garage, crossed the yard with speed surprising in such a fat cat, and disappeared under the bushes around the front porch. What on earth had spooked her? I looked into the shadowy interior, walking slowly now, anxious without formulating exactly why.

The tool-room door was open a crack. Surely Angel and I had shut it the day we'd been in there measuring and straightening.

Angel came out of the side kitchen door and was halfway across the sidewalk between the house and the garage.

I took another step and it seemed to me the crack widened some.

"Angel," I called, panic sparking along my nerves and surely showing in my voice.

She had a reaction that even at the time struck me as extraordinary.

Instead of saying "What?" or "Got a Problem?" she broke into a dead run and moved so fast that she was in front of me one split second after the tool-room door had burst open. The man erupting from it was heading straight for us, and he had our ax in his hands.

"Run!" Angel said fiercely. "Run, Roe!"

That seemed extremely disloyal of me, but also intensely desirable. I couldn't abandon Angel, I decided nobly, idiotically, since the man was swinging the ax and yelling and coming straight for us. Angel ducked under his arm, attempted to grab the ax handle, lost her footing on the loose gravel, and went down. My purse was all I had, and I swung it on its long shoulder strap and had the shock of seeing the ax sever the straps and my purse hit the ground. However, that took up one swing and he had to haul back for another try, and that gave Angel time to lunge from her prone position and grab his ankles, so his next step toward me brought him down as the ax whistled harmlessly past me. He hit the driveway with a thud but kept a grip on the ax, and he was trying to maneuver to use it on Angel when I stomped on his hand.

With a howl he let go of the ax, and I stooped and grabbed the handle and slung it as far away as I could sling. I instinctively wanted the ax out of the equation, since sharp cutting edges make me very nervous. But he used his hands after that, spinning, grabbing Angel's ponytail and hitting her face against the gravel. She did not allow the pain to deflect her, but with an expression of absolute determination reached for a spot on his arm and pressed in with her strong fingers. He screamed and let go, and aimed a kick at Angel's head. Swift as a snake she rolled, and the kick landed on her shoulder instead, but I saw her mouth open in pain. She was slowed down enough for him to jump to his feet. I'd been circling futilely, trying to see a vulnerable spot, but they were so fast it was bewildering. When he jumped up, I insanely tried to block him, but he straightarmed me and my feet in their leather-soled suburban low-heeled pumps flew right out from under me, and with a whump! I landed flat on my back with all my wind knocked out. I was quite unable to move as I heard heavy running steps crunch down the driveway.

Angel's face, scraped and bleeding, appeared over me. "All right?" she asked urgently.

I managed to waggle my head a little, still waiting for the intake of breath that would make me whole.

She ran after the intruder, her footfalls lighter and swifter. But I heard a car start up, and I knew Angel would be back soon.

She was, but in no mood to sit around and rehash our experience.

"Into the house, now!" she said harshly, scooping me off the ground with one movement. I drew in some air finally. The relief was immense. Angel's arm was under mine and I was being dragged/marched into the house. Angel had my damaged purse in her other hand, extracting the keys as we went, and she cast my purse down while she twisted the key in the lock. She more or less pitched me into the living room while she locked the door and shot the deadbolt behind us. While I sat there still trying to figure out what had happened, Angel ran to the kitchen, with blood from the abrasions on her face dropping down to spot the floor.

I heard her voice, quick and calm. She was on the phone calling the police.

I struggled to my feet and wobbled into the kitchen.

Angel was hanging up the phone. She turned to the side kitchen door and shot the deadbolt on it; then the back kitchen door received the same treatment. She went around the kitchen yanking the curtains shut.

Then she turned to me and I realized she was furious. There was nothing slow and deliberate about Angel anymore.

"When I tell you to run, you run," she said in a low, barely controlled voice. "You don't hang around to save my ass. You were in the way out there. I told you to *run*."

"Angel," I said, realization dawning. "You're my *bodyguard*."

We stood staring at one another. Both of us had a lot to think about.

"Why didn't you run?" she asked.

"I couldn't leave you out there." I reached behind me for a towel and handed it to her. "You're dripping all over," I said.

She took it absently and began patting at her face. She glanced down at the towel and seemed surprised at the red blotches on it.

"You have to go to the doctor."

"No," she said. "We'll take care of it. We're not going anywhere until Shelby checks the road between here and town. That's what he's doing now."

"That's who you called."

She nodded. She went to look out the curtains.

"You didn't call the police." I said this cautiously, feeling I was saying something quite naive.

I was right. Angel raised one eyebrow and shook her head.

I didn't even have to ask why. Angel thought this attack was related to Martin's illegal activities. Angel and Shelby, of course, had known all along, I realized in an ever-widening ripple of revelation; Martin had brought them here to protect me before we were even married, had bought me the Julius house because of the garage apartment for the Youngbloods to stay in, had foreseen the possibility that something like this might happen.

I got the first-aid kit from the bathroom, feeling as if I were already half-dead. I was shocked by the attack, humiliated by all I now knew. I should be grateful; I would undoubtedly be dead by now if it weren't for Angel Youngblood. But I felt cold and stony; I hated them all, Angel and Shelby and Martin. I thumped the first-aid kit down on the counter in the kitchen; I picked up the phone. Angel made a face of protest, but before she could speak I turned on her a face so dreadful that she went back to staring out a gap in the curtains.

"Emily," I said, when I heard the voice on the other end of the line, "I won't be able to come to Altar Guild this afternoon, I'm so sorry." Appropriate, but rather huffy, noises from Emily.

"Well, I fell on my way to the garage—yes, I know that's an old-lady thing to do—the gravel was slippery and my shoes are leather-soled—no, I'm fine really, I'm just bruised. I'll be there next time, for sure! Give the ladies my regrets."

I hung up the phone. I stood there, my hand on it, staring off down the black hole I'd fallen into. I got a white washrag out from under the sink, moistened it, wrung it out.

"Sit down," I told Angel.

She abandoned her post but insisted we drag a chair over to the window. She kept watch while I cleaned her face. I knew it hurt; I didn't care. Once her abrasions and cuts were clean, I dabbed antibiotic ointment all over them. She was a sight.

Shelby's car crunched down the drive. He pulled into the Youngbloods' accustomed parking spot on the far side of the garage, so he was hidden from view. Angel had appropriated a knife from my kitchen drawer; she stood watching her husband intently, the knife gripped in her right hand.

"Unlock the kitchen door," she told me.

I did it.

"Stand back from it."

I rolled my eyes and went back to lean against the counter. I could see through Angel's little gap. Finally Shelby crossed it, walking warily, eyes going everywhere at once. In his hands was a shotgun.

My mouth fell open.

A number of things had hit me that day, literally and metaphorically. But the most telling thing, the moment of truth, was seeing that shotgun in Shelby Youngblood's hands.

Someone had tried to kill *me*. That man had been trying to get *me*. Angel had just been an obstacle in his eyes; he'd had no idea of her function or capability. His focus had been on killing me. I thought of that ax coming down on my head. Suddenly my knees were wobbly.

Shelby came in the kitchen door with a rush. Angel was on hand to lock it after him the instant he was in.

"You okay?" he asked her.

She nodded. "Mad," she said. "I'm mad as hell. I couldn't get him. My feet went out from under me. She got the ax away from him, not me." Angel obviously did not need or expect any fuss about her damaged face; Shelby's dark eyes had assessed her injuries quickly and dismissed them. Angel was a professional, it was borne in on me more strongly every minute. If I was dealing with my own humiliation, so was she; she had failed in her job.

"Roe got the ax?" Shelby said incredulously.

"It's in the middle of the front yard. She threw it."

"Roe did." Shelby still couldn't quite absorb it.

"He got very close," Angel said angrily. "If I hadn't already been out of the house, he'd of got her."

I had to sit down quite suddenly.

I pulled one of the breakfast-table chairs out. The legs made a scraping noise.

"So I guess you didn't spot him on your way through town."

"No blue Chevy Nova."

"Tags were covered with mud," Angel said sullenly. I could tell she'd already told Shelby this on the phone and he'd been on the lookout on the way here.

No one could say my married life was placid. No rut for the Bartells!

I giggled.

They glanced at me uneasily, then went back to their consultation.

"It's quiet out there now. We'd better get moving," Shelby said.

"I'll call him," Angel said. She was obviously bent on confessing her failure to someone. After a beat I realized she meant she was going to call Martin, and I just snapped.

"Excuse me," I said viciously. "If anyone is going to call my husband, I am."

They both looked startled at my speaking, and dismayed by what they were hearing.

"You should pack, and talk to Martin tonight," Shelby said gently. But the gentleness was costing him, I could tell. Good.

"I will talk to my husband whenever I damn well please."

They were considerably taken aback. Though I hadn't known the true nature of the Youngbloods, they were finding out a thing or two about me.

They had Martin's telephone numbers where he was staying. They knew where he was and why he was out of town. They knew all about our lives.

They were my bodyguards. I had a little shock whenever the word entered my mind.

Well, Shelby with his acne-scarred face and unruly black hair was nothing like Kevin Costner.

"I will go use the phone in the other room," I told them. I stalked across the hall to sit at Martin's desk and call him in Chicago.

The secretary who took the call was quite sure that Martin's meeting ("He's in conference with the president," she said severely) was more important than my call, but I said, "I really have to insist. This is his wife, and there is an emergency."

After a pause of nearly five minutes, Martin was on the phone, and at the sound of his voice I almost broke down.

"What is it?" he asked tensely. "Are you all right?"

"I'm all right." My voice was shaky. I sat for a moment gathering myself. "Angel is a little hurt," I said with shameful satisfaction.

"Angel? You're all right and *Angel's* hurt? What happened? Is Shelby there?"

"Yes, Martin, Shelby is here and you can talk to him in a minute so you guys can *handle* everything." By golly, I was still mad at everyone. "A man was hiding in the garage, and if he'd had the sense to wait till I was in there, he would've had me. But I noticed something was wrong and he charged out and Angel was able to get there in time, and I got the ax away. But he ran and got in a car and left." Now my voice was shaking again. I certainly wished I could pick an emotion and stick with it. Fear, anger, humiliation, shock. A cocktail of feelings.

"Baby. Are you really all right? Hurt anywhere?"

"Not physically, Martin," I said with great restraint.

"Does Angel need to be in the hospital?"

"No, I took care of it with the first-aid kit."

"That's good. Very good. Okay, honey. Here's what I need you to do. I need you to do whatever Shelby and Angel tell you to do. They're here to keep you safe. I'll catch a flight home tomorrow morning. I'll go to Guatemala once I make sure you're going to be all right."

"Okay," I said tersely. There really wasn't any point in saying anything else.

"Now, I need to talk to Angel and Shelby. I'm— thank God you're okay. I'm so sorry."

I looked across the hall. They were standing close to the kitchen doorway. Shelby had his arms around Angel. A weak moment.

"Phone," I said. "Angel."

Looking as if she'd rather face wrestling an alligator, Angel Youngblood, my protector, came to talk to Martin.

I went upstairs and lay on my bed.

THIRTEEN

IT WAS A LONG NIGHT.

Angel slept in the office/family room downstairs on the couch. Shelby was out patrolling the grounds. I lay awake in our bedroom. Sometimes I read. Sometimes I slept. Sometimes I brooded. In a million years, I could never have imagined myself in the situation in which I found myself now.

I was glad my mother was out of town. I couldn't envision successfully concealing from her all the misery and fear I felt.

Before we'd all gone to our assigned spots for the night, Shelby had questioned us about the appearance of the man. It had all happened quickly, and he'd been in movement the whole time, but I found that if I shut my eyes and replayed him exploding from the tool-room door I could get a fair picture.

"He had on a short-sleeved khaki work shirt," I said first. Angel nodded agreement.

"And safety shoes," Angel contributed, rubbing her shoulder.

"What are safety shoes?" I asked.

"Steel toes," she told me, looking faintly amazed.

"Oh. And he had on dark brown work pants."

"So now we've got his wardrobe. What did he look like?" asked Shelby with very obvious patience.

I had a good mind to stomp up to my room and slam the door, but I was aware that Shelby, of course, was just doing his job and my acting childish would not help the situation. I was sorely tempted, though.

"He had dark curly hair," Angel said.

"He was Angel's height," I contributed. "He was young. Not more than thirty, I doubt that old."

"He does heavy work for a living," Angel said. "Based on his musculature."

"Clean-shaven. Blue eyes, I'm pretty sure. Heavy jaw."

"He never said anything in any language?" Shelby asked us.

"No."

"No."

And that was the sum total of our knowledge of the man in the garage.

THE NEXT MORNING was clear again, definitely hotter. The Youngbloods switched; Shelby went up to their apartment to sleep, and Angel was detailed to stay with me. We ate breakfast and did the dishes in silence, and when we were facing each other dressed in blue jeans and T-shirts, we fidgeted. Angel hadn't gotten her run in. I had finished my last library book, and I was not a daytime television watcher. After one round of the news on CNN, I switched the set off.

Normally, at this time, I would be getting ready to start my round of errands, or at least figuring out what that round should consist of—cleaners, grocery, bank, library—making phone calls, or writing letters. But today I couldn't; they didn't want me to go into town.

"Can we go outside?" I asked Angel finally.

She considered.

"Yes, in the front yard," she said at last. "There are too many trees and bushes that block the view in the backyard."

That was one of the things I liked about it so much.

"In the front yard I can see what's coming," Angel said. "Last night, Shelby took out that clump of bushes out by the road that hid the car."

"He *what?*"

Taken aback, Angel repeated, "He cut down that clump of yellow bells."

"The forsythia is gone," I said unbelievingly. During the night, Shelby had cut down my bushes, a huge beautiful growth of three forsythias that had been happily expanding and blooming for twenty years, I estimated.

"They were down by the road, and they hid things from the house," Angel explained further, puzzled at the degree of my dismay.

"Okay," I said finally. "Okay. Let's go."

"What are we going to do?"

I was punch drunk with lack of sleep and shock.

"Got a Frisbee, Angel?"

"Sure," she said, as though I'd asked her whether she had a nose.

"Well. Let's play Frisbee."

So after a preliminary reconnaissance, we came out into the fresh day. I ignored the shotgun Angel carried out; she put it on the chair on the porch, where she could reach it quickly. Then she got her Frisbee and cocked her wrist to spin it to me, an anticipatory grin stretching her thin lips. I prepared myself for some running.

Ten minutes later I was panting, and even Superwoman was breathing a little heavily. Angel had gotten surprised all over again. I was no mean Frisbee player. But my aerobic exercise videotape hadn't prepared me for this, and I felt the first trickle of sweat for the summer season gliding down my back and then between my hips. On the whole, I was having a good time. I dashed inside for a drink of water.

Angel must have felt mildly challenged. She had backed out toward the road a little, and as I was coming down the front steps, she flicked her wrist and the red disk took off. A sudden breeze gusting over the open field across the road picked up the Frisbee and wafted it even higher. With a thunk, the Frisbee grazed the top of the first roof peak (the roof of the porch) and rolled into the space under my bedroom windows.

"Aw, shit," Angel said. "Listen, I'll be back in a second. Let me go blot my face, the sweat's getting into my scrapes and making them sting."

"Sure," I said. "I'll be getting the ladder."

It felt creepy going into the garage and opening the door to the tool shed in the back. I knew the Young-bloods had checked it out and searched everything on the property before it got dark the night before, but in my brief hours of sleep, I'd had nightmares about a dark figure running toward me with an upraised ax.

I maneuvered the long ladder out of the tool shed and shouldered it to get it to the front of the house. Angel descended the apartment steps with a tender look on her face; the sight of Shelby sleeping certainly still rang her bells.

I pushed back the hooks that held the extension down parallel with the base of the ladder, and with Angel's help ran it up to the roof. Since the house was built up on a high foundation, the climb was no short one.

"Do you mind," Angel said almost shyly, "I know I threw it up there, but if there's one thing I can't handle, it's heights... now if it bothers you, I'll go on and do it, or Shelby can get up there when he gets up..."

I gaped at her, before I remembered my manners and nodded matter-of-factly. "No problem," I said briskly.

She seemed to relax all over. "I'll brace the ladder," she said with equal briskness.

So up I started. I am not automatically afraid of heights; I am fairly phobia-free. But it was quite a climb, and since I was showing off for Angel, I found

I needed to keep my eyes looking up and my progress steady. Stopping, I had a strong feeling, would not be good.

Actually—come to think of it—I had never been on a roof before. The porch roof was steep. Really steep. Nervously, I transferred from the ladder to the shingles, already warm from the spring sun. I'd never been right next to shingles before; I had a good look at their pebbly grayness while I was bracing myself to reach the peak. I stretched and grasped it, and pushed with the sides of my feet, glad I was wearing sturdy rubber-soled hi-tech sneakers. The Frisbee should be on the downslope of this roof, where it joined the roof of the house; I remembered Miss Neecy telling me about the feuding couple who'd built the house, Sarah May Zinsner's last-minute insistence on a porch.

"I hear a car coming, Roe," Angel said quietly down below.

I froze. "What should I do?"

"Get over that roofline."

So I scrambled up and over in no time at all. A little incentive was all I needed. In the valley between the two roofs, formed like a forty-five-degree angle with the wall under my bedroom windows being the straight line and the upward slope of the porch roof being the angle line, lay the bright red Frisbee and an old gray tarp so exactly matching the shingles that I had to land on it to notice it.

I peeked over the roofline to see what Angel was doing. The shotgun was in her hands now, and she was against the inside of the wall of the garage, the far side where Martin's Mercedes was parked. The car was visible coming closer, thanks to Shelby's butchery of my forsythia, and it was a white car that was a little familiar. It turned in the driveway, and Angel raised the shotgun. The white car crunched slowly up the drive and pulled to a halt on the gravel a few feet behind my car, in the near side of the garage. The driver's door opened. Martin stepped out.

I was smiling without even realizing it for a second.

Angel came out of the garage with the shotgun lowered, and though I couldn't hear what they said, she pointed at the roof.

"Up here!" I called. Martin turned and went to the front of the house, looking up with a quizzical expression. He wasn't wearing a suit for once, and he needed a shave.

"How are you, Roe?" he asked.

I still loved him.

"I'm all right, Martin. Be down in a minute. Here's the Frisbee." I sailed it over the peak down to them. Martin's arm shot out and he caught it neatly.

"There's something else up here," I called. "There's a gray plastic tarp."

Angel's expression changed to alarm. "Don't touch it!" she and Martin yelled simultaneously.

"It's been here for ages," I reassured them. "There're pine needles and bird poop and dirt all over it."

The two faces upturned to me relaxed somewhat.

"What do you think it is, builder's material?" Martin asked.

"Well, I'm going to find out." I maneuvered a turn in the little valley in which I found myself. A gutter had been installed in this valley, to carry off rainwater, and the covered bundle had been shoved just clear of it under my bedroom window. In fact it was so closely packed into this one straight stretch of roof that I knew why I hadn't ever noticed it: It was so close under my window that I would have had to stick out my head and shoulders and look down to see it.

The tarp was stiff and crackly with age and exposure. It was weighted down with bricks. When I shoved one of the tarp and raised one corner, the whole thing moved, and I was treated to a comprehensive view of what lay beneath.

It took me a moment to understand what I was seeing. I tried to believe that someone had been up on the roof eating ribs and had thrown the discarded bones in a heap after he was through. Maybe lots of people; there were so many...I saw the ribs first, you see. They weren't pretty and white: they were yellowish and had little bits of dried dark stuff on them. But there were other bones, tiny and large, one whole hand with a few strings of tendon still holding it together...the skulls had rolled a little, but I counted them automatically.

"Roe?" Martin called from below. "What's happening up there? Are you okay?"

The breeze was gusting again. For the first time in over six years, it wafted under the gray plastic. The hair on one of the skulls lifted.

I wanted *off this roof*.

I flung myself upward, swung my legs over the peak, and began backing down in record time.

"Roe," called Martin again, definitely alarmed.

My feet hit the first rung. It seemed like long minutes before my hands could grasp the metal and then my feet flew down once I was totally supported by the ladder.

Martin and Angel were both asking me questions at once. I leaned against the metal, my feet finally on the ground, a safe distance from the horror on the roof.

"They're there," I managed to say at last. "They've been there all along."

Martin still looked blank, but Angel, who had helped me look, got the point immediately.

"The Julius family," she told Martin. "They're on the roof."

WE DID HAVE to tell the police about this. Angel stored away the shotgun and made the phone calls. Then I saw her bounding up her apartment steps, presumably to wake Shelby.

We were sitting on the porch in one of the chairs. I was folded up on Martin's lap.

"Martin," I whispered. "She still had on her wig. But there was just a skull underneath it."

EVERYONE CAME. It was like a lawn party for law enforcement personnel in Spalding County.

Our house was just within the city limits, so the chief of police came first. Padgett Lanier was sharp-nosed, tall, with thinning blond hair and nearly invisible eyelashes and eyebrows. He had a paunch, and a mouth that was too small for his face. He had been chief of police of Lawrenceton for twenty years. I'd met him at various parties while I was dating Arthur Smith.

I was sitting in a separate chair by then, but still on the porch, hoping to keep everyone out of our home. Martin had pulled his chair over by mine and was holding my hand. Shelby and Angel were sitting on the porch itself, blocking the front door, watching the activity with impassive faces.

"Mrs. Bartell?" Lanier asked from the front lawn.

"Ms. Teagarden," I said.

"You the one that found them?"

"Yes. They're up on the roof. Under the plastic."

"The picture man should be here in a minute," he said. It sounded as though he were talking about Mr. Rogers; Padgett Lanier was one of those people who think because I'm small, I'm childlike. "I'd better let him go up first. Did you touch anything while you were up there, honey? How'd you happen to go up on the roof? Wait, here comes Jack; you might as well tell both of us at once."

Detective Sergeant Jack Burns came next, and I heaved a sigh when I saw him emerge from his car. He hated my guts. On the other hand, he treated me like an adult. Burns was wearing one of his hideous suits, which he apparently bought at garage sales held on dark nights. He stood looking at the ladder with a face even grimmer than usual. He did not relish making the climb. His no-color hair was scantier than when I'd last seen him, and the flesh of his face was sagging.

Lynn Liggett Smith was right behind him, looking as slim, tall, and competent as ever, and she had the "picture man" with her. Several other cars pulled in after Lynn's, and it began to seem that whoever was off duty or had decided they weren't needed at the moment had driven out to the Julius place to see what was happening. It was the place to be if you were a cop.

Martin murmured, "Is there no other crime in this town that needs investigating? Surely somebody is running a stop sign somewhere."

"Most of them, probably, were here six years ago," I said.

After a thoughtful moment, he nodded.

Padgett Lanier conferred with Jack Burns, and the picture man was dispatched up the ladder first. Lynn went up after him to help carry his equipment. Fortunately, she was wearing slacks. She looked through the rungs at me on her way. She shook her head slightly, as if I'd gotten up to another naughty trick.

The yard fell silent. All the policemen—and aside from Lynn, they were all male—looked up at the roof above our heads. I could hear the scrape of the photographer's shoes as he scrambled up the roof; the pause as he reached the top, saw the tarp. He said something to Lynn; I heard her reply, "Here," as she handed him his camera from her place on the ladder. I could only see her feet from my chair. Presumably he took a few pictures. I heard him say, "Lift the tarp for me, Detective," and then Lynn's progress across the roof. I swear I heard the rattle of the stiff, cracking plastic as Lynn raised it.

"They're stacked on top of each other, Martin," I murmured. "I guess it's all three of them."

"Mostly bones, Roe?" Martin asked. His face was calm, and I knew he was being matter-of-fact because he knew I needed it. And because he had seen death far more often than I.

"Yes . . . mostly. The wig is on her skull. I told you that. I don't understand about the wig."

"Probably a synthetic."

"No, no. It's the wrong wig."

His eyes were questioning and he leaned closer, but at that moment Lynn came down the ladder, turned to her superiors, and nodded curtly.

"Three of them," she said. "Three skulls, anyway."

A collective sigh seemed to go up from the people on my front lawn.

"Jerry's going to pass the tarp down," she said. "Then he'll take more pictures." She went to her car and got a large plastic garbage bag. She beckoned to a patrolman. He sprang to help, and they spread the mouth of the garbage bag wide. There were a series of scraping sounds as the photographer/policeman removed the tarp.

"Need someone up here to pass it down!" he called.

Jack Burns shambled forward to the foot of the ladder and began to climb heavily. He had pulled on plastic gloves.

They made an effort to pass the tarp down folded, so nothing would spill from its surface, but it was cracking with age and a few pieces had to be retrieved from the bushes around the porch. Finally it was sealed in the garbage bag and placed in Lynn's car.

"Get whoever's on dispatch to call Morrilton Funeral Home to come out here. Tell them what to expect," she told the patrolman who'd helped hold the bag. He nodded and went to his patrol car radio.

Some of the men approached Lynn with a request, and after a moment's thought, she nodded. They converged at the foot of the ladder. One by one the men climbed up. We would hear the scrape of heavy official shoes, a silence as he peeked over the porch roof, then he would come down. The process would be repeated. While that was going on, Lynn and her two superiors congregated on the porch. Shelby got up and arranged three chairs facing ours. Angel took Martin's chair. He and Shelby stood on the side of the porch, where Angel and I could see them. This did not suit Jack Burns, I could tell, but he could hardly tell our husbands to leave when Angel and I were innocent bystanders to another family's tragedy.

"Could we move inside?" he asked, with as much geniality as he could muster.

Angel had actually shifted in her seat preparatory to rising when I said, "I'd really rather not." She shot me a startled look and tried to settle back as though she'd never moved. I saw from the corner of my eye that Martin had blinked in surprise, and Shelby turned to one side to hide a grin.

Lynn, Lanier, and Jack Burns all looked surprised, too.

I didn't want my house invaded.

"Well, it is a right nice day out here," Lanier said smoothly.

"How did you come to go up on the roof, Roe?" Lynn asked.

"Angel and I were playing Frisbee."

Lanier looked from Angel to me, comparing our sizes, and put his hand over his mouth to shield his smile.

"Angel threw the Frisbee, there was a gust of wind, and it ended up going up on the roof. I got the ladder, climbed up, got the Frisbee, and found—them."

"You were there, Mrs. Youngblood?" Lynn asked politely.

"I was holding the ladder. I'm scared of heights."

"What happened to your face, young lady?" Jack Burns asked, in tones of tender solicitousness.

"I fell on the gravel driveway, and I couldn't catch myself in time," Angel said. Her hands, resting on the arms of the chair, were perfectly relaxed.

"And you, Mr. Bartell?" Lynn asked suddenly, swinging around in her seat to look at Martin. "Where were you when your wife went up on the roof? And Mr. Youngblood?"

"I was driving in from the airport. I got here while my wife was up on the roof," Martin responded. "I've been away on a business trip."

"I was asleep," Shelby said.

"You're not working today?"

"I felt sick this morning, and didn't go in. As a matter of fact, I started feeling real bad yesterday afternoon, all of a sudden. I came home from work then and haven't been back since."

Shelby had neatly covered his sudden departure from work yesterday afternoon after Angel had called him. A "just in case" move, I thought.

That was really all Lynn could ask us, given the circumstances. Perhaps it was even one or two questions more than she should have asked us, come to think about it.

"I'm taking my wife inside now, she's had a shock," Martin said. The police cars were vanishing one by one, but local people were beginning to drive by; someone had been listening to the scanner. A hearse from Morrilton Funeral Home pulled into our driveway, and abruptly I could hardly wait to be inside the house.

There was no reason for me to stay, so Lynn nodded. Shelby and Angel came in with us. Martin pulled the drape cord in the living room and blocked out the cruising cars and the police and the funeral-home men. But nothing could block out the sounds from the roof.

FOURTEEN

I WANTED THE Youngbloods to go to their apartment. I wanted to forget about the mad ax-man and the bones on the roof. I wanted to watch an old movie on the TV, curled up on the couch with a big bowl of popcorn and maybe a beer. I wanted Martin upstairs after the movie was over. Or even earlier.

But his agenda was different, I realized with a sigh.

He gathered us around the table in the kitchen.

"Now, what happened yesterday?" he asked.

I told him again, and then Angel began her part, her battered face more testimony than her words.

I slumped back in my chair sullenly. A night short on sleep and two days of violent emotions were taking their toll. I was very tired and very sick of crises. I wanted this all to go away, just for a little while, so I could make one of my slow adjustments. But of course I was thinking again of the man who had run at me, and now that I was too tired to be scared, I thought more of his face. While Martin was saying something about security to the Youngbloods, something about the bushes, I realized that there had been something faintly familiar about the man. I associated him with construction, building....

The phone rang. I went to the counter to answer it. Sally Allison wanted to know all about the skeletons on the roof; she was not in her "friend" mode, but in her "reporter" mode. I told her.

"You know," she said, "the police will call in the forensic anthropologist on this one. Did you know Georgia is the only state with a forensic anthropologist on the payroll? He's never been called to a case in Spalding County before! He'll be here tomorrow."

"Wouldn't it be funny," I said, "if it wasn't the Juliuses?"

Dead silence. Then Sally laughed uncertainly. "Who else could it be, Roe?" she asked, as carefully as though she were speaking to a lunatic.

I thought, If I were rested I could figure this out, something important. "Never mind," I said. "See you later, Sally." I hung up, and the phone rang again. I dealt with that call. Then another. Finally, I switched off the sound and turned on the answering machine.

I sat down at the table with the others, who had been conferring in low voices all this time.

"Roe," Martin began, and I knew he was about to tell me what to do.

"Martin," I interrupted. "I think Angel and I will take a few days off and fly to New Orleans."

They all gaped at me. It was very gratifying.

"I know you need to go to Guatemala, and I expect Shelby needs to be getting back to work before the other people at the plant start to ask questions, so the best thing, with the phone ringing off the wall and all, would be for me—and Angel, since you think I need a bodyguard—to just go somewhere. And I think we might go to New Orleans. It's been years since I was there."

Martin looked suspicious. But he said, "That sounds good, Roe. Angel, how does that sound to you?"

"Suits me," Angel said cautiously. "I can pack and be ready to go in thirty minutes."

"That would give me a chance to look into having some security installed here," Shelby said.

"I don't want to find an armed fortress when I come back," I told him.

He did not even look at Martin; give him credit for that. "I won't do anything until I talk to you both," he said.

I nodded and stood up in a very pronounced way. The Youngbloods rose instantly and left for their apartment. Martin went to the living room and looked through the crack in the drapes.

"They're leaving," he said, not turning around. "All the police. The hearse has gone."

I waited.

He finally faced me. "Roe, I don't know what to tell you now. Nothing has turned out as we planned. I wanted a good life for us, I wanted to provide for you and take care of you and I never wanted any harm or upset to come to you. I thought I could keep the gun thing separate. I thought I would go to work at the plant and come home and you would tell me about whatever you were interested in and I would enjoy it and we would make love every night."

Maybe I had sort of planned on all that, too.

"Well, Martin. It looks like we're not going to have that, exactly." I walked over and put my arms around him, lay my head against his chest. He squeezed me so hard I thought I would squeak. "We'll have something different, though. If you can disentangle yourself from this arms thing..." we have a chance, I finished silently. "But," I resumed, "we can still go for part of your expectations."

"Hmm?"

"We can make love every night."

"Let's go upstairs."

"Good idea."

Readers, he carried me.

NEW ORLEANS. In New Orleans, Angel's battered face attracted little attention. Angel followed me grimly through the gorgeous new Aquarium of the Americas at the foot of Canal Street. Angel sulkily refused iced coffee and *beignets* at the Cafe du Monde. Angel accepted the rooms and the service at the Hyatt Regency with calm disdain. When a tattooed man on Bourbon Street grabbed my arm and made a suggestion so bizarre and indecent that my jaw dropped open, Angel stepped up from behind me, pressed his arm in a particular spot right above his elbow, and glanced back with grim satisfaction while he rubbed his useless arm and cursed.

"Why are we really here?" she asked after I'd bought my mother some antique earrings at a little shop in the French Quarter.

"Let's go on the walking tour of the cemetery," I suggested. We met the tour guide at a little cafe close to the police station. The cafe was loaded with charm and fancy versions of coffee. The guide was also loaded with charm, if an offbeat brand, and I found myself as curious about his sex life as I was about the tour, which was very interesting—though I can't say Angel seemed too impressed. After we'd received the lecture about staying with the group since there'd been some muggings in the cemetery, I saw from Angel's restive gaze and alert stance that she was aching for someone to try to attack us.

"Why are we really here?" she asked, as we ate in a Cajun restaurant across from the convention center.

"Let's go to the zoo tomorrow," I suggested.

When we got back to the Hyatt, I found Martin had left a voice message on my room telephone. "I'm here, I'm trying hard, and it looks possible but difficult," he said. "I miss you more than I can say." I had a sudden blur of tears in my eyes and sat on the side of my bed gripping a Kleenex.

It wasn't the message I'd hoped for. Dawdling in New Orleans, having a good time, wasn't going to work. I was going to have to try Plan B.

I should have called Sally Allison. It would have helped a lot. But frankly, it never occurred to me.

"Tomorrow, Angel," I said, "we're going to work."

"About damn time."

FIFTEEN

ANGEL WAS DRIVING. She was very comfortable and competent behind the wheel. She'd opened up enough to tell me she'd taken several driving courses especially for bodyguards. We were going out to Metairie, a giant suburb of New Orleans, where Melba Totino had lived with her sister before she'd moved to Lawrenceton.

There was a phone listing for Mrs. Totino's sister, Alicia Manigault, in the Metairie phone book.

Mrs. Totino had gotten all misty when she spoke of her former home, but I couldn't see much about Metairie to love, from the interstate, anyway. There were hundreds of small houses jammed into tiny lots, charmless and styleless, leavened by an occasional motel or restaurant or strip shopping center. Surely there were prettier parts of Metairie somewhere?

The heat had begun in earnest here, and I shuddered when I thought of what it must be like in July or August. We had the air-conditioning on in the rental car, and I still felt sticky when we got out on the short, narrow street where Alicia Manigault lived. Scrubby stunted palms were planted here and there in tiny yards. All the houses were very small and one story, and though some of them were spick and span, others were in need of repair and paint. I would hate living in a place like this more than anything I could imagine. I felt very there-but-for-the-grace-of-God.

The squat flat-roofed house at the phone book address was moderately well cared for. The grass was mowed, but there were no ornamental touches to the yard, beyond some straggly foundation bushes. The house, formerly barn red, was peeling, and the side facing the afternoon sun was noticeably lighter than the rest of the house.

Angel unfolded herself from the dark green rental car and surveyed the street expressionlessly. "What do you want to do?" she asked.

"Ring the doorbell."

The whole property was enclosed in a low chain-link fence. The gate creaked.

There didn't seem to be a doorbell, so I knocked instead. My heart was beating uncomfortably.

A young woman answered.

I had never seen her before. She was very fat, very fair, wearing a pink dollar-store "Plus-Size" muumuu.

"What you want?" she asked. She didn't look unfriendly, just busy.

"Is Mrs. Manigault here?" I asked.

"Alicia? No, she's not here."

"She doesn't live here?"

"Well, it's her house," the young woman said, her small blue eyes blinking in a puzzled way behind blue-framed glasses.

"And you rent it from her," Angel said.

"My husband and me, yeah, we do. What you want with Alicia?" A strange sound behind her made the young woman turn her head.

"Listen, come on in," she said. "I got a sick dog in here."

We followed her into the tiniest living room I had ever seen. It was jammed with vinyl furniture covered with crocheted afghans in a variety of patterns. The only thing they had in common was a stunningly dreadful combination of colors. Angel and I gaped.

"I know," the woman said, with a little laugh, "everyone just cain't believe it. I sell them at craft shows on the weekend, but the ones in here are my favorites. I just couldn't sell them. My husband always says, "You'd think we got cold here!"

She bent over a basket in the corner by a doorway into, I thought, the kitchen. When she straightened, she had in her arms a tiny black dog with brown on its muzzle—a Toy Manchester, I thought.

"Kickapoo," she said proudly. "That's his name."

Angel made a snorting noise and I realized she was trying not to laugh. I was too concerned by the obvious illness of the dog. It was limp and listless in her arms.

"What's the matter?" I asked, not at all sure I really wanted to know.

"He got hurt," she said. "A bad man kicked our little doggy two days ago, didn't he, Kickapoo?"

"Oh, that's terrible!"

"Kickapoo couldn't hurt anyone, you can see that," said the woman, dreadful indignation printed deep in folds of fat. "I don't know what was the matter with him." I assumed she was referring to the kicker. "He was in a bad mood that day, but he never has done nothing like that."

"Not your husband?" I inquired incredulously.

"Oh, no! Carl loves our little doggy," she said, "doesn't he, Kickapoo?"

The dog didn't nod.

"No, this was a friend of Alicia's, the man she has collect the rent and tend to things for her. 'Course, we mow the lawn and take care of the little repairs, but if something big goes wrong, we call..." and she stopped dead.

"Yes?" I said encouragingly. I was totally bored with the conversation until the woman so obviously remembered she wasn't supposed to be having it.

"Nothing. Here I am, going on and on. I haven't even found out what you need."

Angel and I were both well-dressed that day, since I thought that'd be reassuring to an old lady like Alicia Manigault. I was wearing a little suit with a white jacket and a navy skirt, and Angel had on tailored black slacks and a sapphire blue blouse with a gold chain and earrings. So it wasn't out of the question for Angel to claim we were from the Metairie Senior Citizens' Association, which she promptly did.

"Oh," the woman said. "I never heard of that. But that's nice."

"And you're Mrs.—?" Angel said pointedly.

The woman reached for an eyedropper by a bottle of medicine on a table jammed into one end of the living room. She squeezed what was in it into the little dog's mouth. It swallowed obediently.

"Coleman," she said, looking down at the animal. "Lanelda Coleman."

"So Mrs. Manigault doesn't need transportation services to and from the center?" Angel asked.

"No, she's just here a few weeks a year," Lanelda Coleman told us.

I was totally at sea.

I opened my mouth to ask where she was the rest of the year, but my cohort kicked me in the ankle.

"Then we'll just go, I can tell you've got your hands full," Angel said sympathetically.

"Oh," Lanelda said, "I do. We're just terrified Kickapoo is hurt bad. We've about decided to take him to the vet. It's so expensive!"

I moved restlessly. They adored the dog but hadn't taken him to the vet?

"It sure is," Angel agreed.

"Carl and I just were up all night with this little thing," Lanelda said abstractedly, her attention on the dog.

"The man who kicked him should pay for the vet visit," Angel said.

I turned to stare at her.

Lanelda's face looked suddenly determined. "You know, lady, you're right," she said. "I'm gonna call him the minute Carl gets home."

"Good luck," I said, and we left.

We conferred by the car.

"We need to ask some questions," I said.

"But not of her. She's been told not to talk about the arrangements for that house by someone, someone she's scared of. We don't want her calling whoever it is and telling them we've been asking questions."

"So what do we do?"

"We move the car," Angel said slowly. "Then we go from house to house. Her curtains are closed, and she's busy with the dog. She may not notice. Our cover story is that we're canvassing old people in the neighborhood about the need for a community center with hot meals and transportation to and from this center every day. I just hope Metairie doesn't have one already. Ask questions about the old ladies who own Number Twenty-one."

I looked up at Angel admiringly. "Good idea."

I WASN'T SO enthusiastic an hour later. I'd never knocked on strangers' doors before. We'd waited until after five o'clock so people would be home; most of the mothers here would be working mothers.

This was an experience that I later wanted to forget. I was never intended to be a private detective; I was too thin-skinned. The old people were suspicious, the younger people were too busy at this time of day to give much thought to my questions, or could think of no good reason why they should spend time talking to a stranger. I actually had a door or two shut in my face.

One woman in her sixties, Betty Lynn Sistrump, did remember the sisters when they were in residence, and had known them superficially.

"I was amazed when Alicia told me Melba had moved out," Mrs. Sistrump said. She was wearing a bathrobe and a lot of makeup for a woman her age—or any age. "They were like Siamese twins or somethin'. Always together, though they sure fought sometimes."

"So you don't think Mrs. Totino lives anywhere in Metairie?" I asked, to keep up the fiction. "We need to contact her about the center, if she does."

"Alicia said she was going back up to somewhere up north—Georgia, I think—to live with her daughter."

"Do you remember about when that was?" I managed to say. I'd been struck almost speechless at the thought of Georgia being far north to this woman. Georgia, north! If my hair had been shorter, it would've bristled.

When Mrs. Sistrump opined it'd been about five years, more or less, since she'd talked to Alicia—though she'd caught glimpses of her since then going into and out of the house—she admitted it had caused her no grief, not seeing the sister. And that was the impression I'd gotten from all the people on the street who would actually talk to me.

Flattened by the whole experience, I returned to the rental car to find Angel leaning against it staring off into space. Angel had a great quality of repose.

"Carl's home," she said. "It must be him. He went in without knocking."

It took me a few seconds to track that down mentally.

"Okay," I said cautiously.

"Lanelda said," Angel reminded me, "that when Carl came home, she would talk to him about calling the man who'd kicked their dog. And that's the man who must know where Alicia Manigault is."

"So what do we do?" I asked uncertainly.

"I can try to creep in there under the windows and listen," Angel said dubiously. "Or we can just wait and see if the man comes. He'd have to to give them the money for the vet visit, wouldn't he?"

"Sounds pretty iffy. What if the dog died this afternoon? What if the man says he won't give a dime?"

"Got a better idea?"

Well, we could go back to our luxurious hotel and order a great meal. But that wasn't why we were here, I told myself.

It was still light, but fading fast. While we waited for it to get darker, so Angel could gauge if she could risk her creep, we drove to the nearest fast-food place. While we dealt with French fries and chicken sandwiches in the rental car, we exchanged stories about our block canvas.

Of the people Angel had talked to, only two households remembered the sisters. The other people had moved in since Alicia had rented the house. The two accounts Angel had pieced together basically matched Betty Lynn Sistrump's. About six years before, Alicia had told people who cared enough to inquire that her sister had gone to live with her daughter. Soon after that, Alicia had rented the house and had only appeared from time to time since then. One alert woman, confined to a wheelchair and dependent on neighborhood happenings for her entertainment, remembered a police car visiting the house about then—an occurrence so unusual that she'd asked Alicia about it, the next time she'd seen her.

"And got my head bit off for asking," she'd told Angel. "I guess I was just being nosy, but wouldn't you be? I mean, what if she'd had a robbery or a prowler? Those are things other people in the same neighborhood need to know about, aren't they?"

"And she never asked you why a do-gooder trying to find out if Alicia Manigault needed a ride to a senior citizens' center would need to know that?"

"Nope," Angel said, simply. "She just wanted someone to talk to. And she wanted to know if the bus that would take them was equipped to handle wheelchairs. I had to tell her the whole thing was still pretty much up in the air. She was disappointed."

We looked away from each other, off into the distance. Angel drank the last of her Coke. Spenser and Hawk we weren't; not even Elvis Cole and Joe Pyle.

"What do you think, is it dark enough?" I asked.

"Yep. But I've been looking at that yard, and I don't think there's a single place I could get that I wouldn't be visible from at least four other houses."

"Um. You're right."

"So we better just watch for a while. Maybe he'll come. Whoever he is."

In the short time it had taken to collect our food, return, and eat, the character of the neighborhood had changed. More cars were home; the little street was jammed with people who'd had to park at the curb. The streetlights had come on in the deep dusk and cast sharp-contrast shadows. There were some children outside playing. Angel was right, creeping around that little property was out of the question in a neighborhood as congested as this one. It was hard to see how we could sit and observe, even. How did police stake out places like this? Surely, if we started moving and kept driving by, someone would eventually get suspicious.

We left for a minute, and pulled in down the street a little, in front of a house that was still dark and had no vehicles in the driveway. We looked at our watches and shook our heads; pantomime of people waiting impatiently. Then Angel watched in the rear-view mirror and I watched the side mirror.

"I thought you were used to this, Angel," I said.

"How come?"

"You used to be a bodyguard."

"Then, I was watching out for people like me. I was trying to find anyone waiting for my employer. I never waited for anyone."

"Oh. What happened to your last client? Martin never told me."

Angel diverted her eyes from the mirror to look at me directly. "And for good reason," she said. "Believe me, you don't want to know."

I had a feeling she was right.

Sooner than we had any right to expect, our vigil was rewarded. Carl must have been persuasive or righteous over the phone. A pickup squealed up, a white one with a fancy pattern of fuchsia and green flames painted trailing down the side.

"Don't know where he can park," Angel muttered. "There's only one spot left on the whole street, and that's right in front of us...Shit, was I stupid! Get down!" The pickup did indeed maneuver into the space against the curb ahead of our rental car. The driver would have to walk right past us.

I dove down onto the floor board and compressed myself into as tiny a ball as possible. Angel, as usual, had had her hair pulled back in a ponytail; now she yanked out the band that held it, fluffed her hair quickly, and unfolded our New Orleans map with hasty fingers. She held the map up, partially obscuring her face, where the bruises were fading and there were only a few scabs left.

I heard the pickup door slam and heavy steps pass quickly by the car.

"Is he going to their house?" I whispered.

"Shut up! Yes!"

After a long moment, Angel said, "Okay, you can sit up. He's inside."

"Did you get a good look at him?"

"Yeah." She had the strangest expression as she gathered up her hair and bound it back into her customary ponytail.

"So?"

"It was the man who tried to kill us."

THE AX-MAN, somehow in league with Melba Totino and her sister Alicia? So he wasn't in any way involved with my husband's Latin American ventures; we could safely have called the police when he attacked us. We could be on the right side of the law, instead of Martin's side.

"So. We follow him?" Angel asked.

"I guess so," I said. "Can you figure this out?"

Angel shook her head. But she wasn't unconcerned; her mouth was compressed into an even thinner line. Her hands gripped the steering wheel until her knuckles turned white. She hadn't liked being beaten, she hadn't liked having been so close to losing her client, she hadn't liked having to tell Martin or her husband about what had happened, and on a personal level, I suspected she really hadn't liked having her face messed up.

From being basically indifferent about what she considered a personal obsession of mine, Angel had graduated to being vitally interested in the Julius case. So we both watched eagerly for the man's emergence from the little house.

"We better not be here when he comes out again," Angel said, and she started the car. We drove around the block until we were positioned on a cross street so that when he came out, we would be able to fall in behind him unless he did something crazy, like attempting a U-turn on the narrow, crowded street.

I was able to see him for the first time when he shut the door of Alicia Manigault's house behind him. He was tall and muscular, and he looked younger than I'd remembered him. He wore jeans and a work shirt, with the sleeves rolled up. His hair was dark and curly, and he was clean-shaven; Angel and I had been good witnesses. It was hard to square this all-American blue-collar hunk with the maniac waving an ax who'd so nearly mowed me down a few days before.

"He's walking a little stiff," Angel said happily. "I think we banged him around some."

"I hope so."

He strode to his lurid pickup truck and started it up.

We drove out of Metairie and across the Huey P. Long Bridge and went south steadily. After at least twenty miles, he turned right, and we followed him. He didn't seem to be looking out for cars following him, or for anything else.

"An amateur," Angel muttered. I couldn't tell if she was pleased by our attacker's amateurism, or disgusted, or enraged. If it was difficult following him at night, she didn't say so.

Now we were on a narrow road with a bayou on one side, houses on the other. There were boats lining the bayou, with signs for swamp tours, promising alligators and abundant wildlife. Most of the signs featured the word "Cajun." The lighting wasn't good, but the white truck with the bright blazes painted on the side was fairly easy to spot. Finally it slowed and turned into one of the narrow driveways. We had to drive on past, and I stared as hard as I could in the dark to see a sort of cabin with a screened-in front porch. Ax-man had parked the truck under a carport, which the truck shared with a battered blue Chevy Nova and a tarp-covered boat.

"That's the car he was driving in Georgia," Angel said.

We drove on until we came to a juke joint, where Angel pulled in and parked. We looked at each other questioningly.

Neither of us knew what to do next.

"We could watch all night, or we could come back tomorrow, or we could call Shelby from a pay phone in there." Angel nodded her head towards the bar, from which came loud zydeco music and a fairly constant flow of in-and-out traffic. I wasn't about to go in there.

"Let's find out more before we call Shelby," I said. "I want to know who lives in that house."

SIXTEEN

IT RAINED the next morning, steamy relentless rain that made the inside of the rental car damp and sticky despite the air-conditioner. We went from the Hyatt Regency in urban New Orleans to the cabin in rural south Louisiana, a sort of cultural leap that sat better with Angel than it did with me. By the time we got there, the truck was gone, but the old Nova was still parked where it had been the night before.

There were neighbors close to this cabin; lots facing the bayou were as valuable as waterfront property anywhere, especially since most of the people along this stretch of road apparently made their living giving tourists swamp tours. On the other hand, since tourists were common, we didn't stick out as obviously as we might have. A tiny souvenir shop sitting cheek-by-jowl with a boat tour departure site was already open. The man inside, dressed in camouflage greens and browns, his rough black hair in tousled waves, looked like a refugee from a Rambo movie. Angel put on some lipstick and slid from the car. "He's more my type," she told me. "I'll see what I can find out." The rain had settled down to a very light drizzle.

She'd left her elastic band off this morning, and her blond hair fluffed prettily around her narrow face. In a pair of tight jeans, a sleeveless T-shirt, and sneakers, she could stop traffic if she chose, and this morning, she did choose. She sauntered up to the service window of the little shack, rested her elbows on the sill, and within a minute was deep in conversation with the dark-haired man, whose white teeth flashed in a constant grin. Angel was smiling, shrugging, tossing back her hair, and in general behaving atypically. But it seemed to be quite effective. When she started back to the car, she turned around several times to call back, as he extended the conversation.

"Whoo," she said in relief, as she slid into her seat. "Talk about Cajun! He had an accent so thick you could cut it, and could charm the birds from the trees, too."

"What did he say?"

"I told him this long story... I'd met this guy in a bar last night, and I didn't know his name, but he had this really distinctive truck and lived somewhere right about here. And then I said I'd lost the napkin with his name and phone number, but I was trying to track him down before he called me, because I suspected he was married. And I wanted to know for sure before I went out with him."

"And?"

"This guy in the souvenir booth wanted me to forget about the man I'd met last night and go out with him instead, but I told him I'd promised the man I'd meet him tonight, though I'd shove him off if he was married." Angel made a circular sweep with her hand to indicate how long this badinage had taken her. "What it all boils down to—the ax-man is renting this cabin, has been for a couple of years now. No one owns a house along this road that isn't Cajun, by the way, because of some law that the houses go to family members and no one ever sells, but this particular house, the only son is in the Army right now and just wants someone to live in it until he comes back from his tour of duty—or something like that."

"Did you get a name?"

"The name is apparently Dumont, or something like that. He works at the lumber yard not five minutes from here. And he is married; or at least there's a woman in residence, and Rene said he's heard she's pretty ferocious. He advised me to keep clear."

"I don't know what to do now," I observed, after we'd looked at each other a moment or two. "Why would a man named Dumont attack us with an ax? Why is he the rent collector for Alicia Manigault? Where is she? She can't be dead, if she appears for a few weeks each year and crams herself into that house with the Colemans and the dog."

"And what does it all have to do with the bodies on the roof of the house, as long as we're asking questions?" Angel added. "All I know to do is ask someone who might know the answer."

I thought long and hard to find a way around that, but it did seem as if that was the only way to do it. At least the ax-man was gone, and maybe we could find out something in his absence that would explain his attack on us. What we were going to do about it once we discovered the reason, I hadn't the faintest notion.

"Someone comes running at me with an ax, I want to know why," Angel said. She was looking at me sideways, sensing my hesitation.

This was a point of pride for Angel.

"Let's go knock on the door," I said.

WE RECONNOITERED briefly. There were no cars at the houses on either side of the cabin. We looked at each other and shrugged.

I pulled boldly into the driveway. I was driving, with Angel crouched on the floorboards. I parked as close as possible behind the old car, so the passenger door was not as visible from the front window. As soon as I'd gone inside with the woman, providing as much distraction as possible, Angel was to slip from the car and snake around back. There were enough bushes in the yard to provide cover. If the air-conditioner wasn't already on, maybe there'd be a window open so Angel could hear if I got into trouble.

This was pretty close to having no plan at all.

My palms were sweating as I got out of the rental car. It was still raining enough to keep the tourists away, and the Bayou Cajun Boat Tour place across the road was deserted. I clamped my purse under one arm as if it were a friend, and I marched up to the cabin, creaked across the screened-in porch, and rang the doorbell.

I was prepared for the woman who answered the door to be tough, perhaps cheap-looking and foulmouthed. Though very nervous, I was braced.

But I was not ready for the door to be answered by a dead woman.

"Yes?" said Charity Julius.

She thought much more quickly than I, no doubt about it.

The expression on my face and the gasp I gave left no doubt in her mind that she was recognized. She didn't know who the hell I was, but she knew I recognized her.

About the time Angel was gliding around the side of the house on her way to the back, Charity Julius punched me in the stomach hard enough to double me over, and while I was bent, she brought her clenched fists down in a vicious blow to the back of my neck. By the time Angel was at the kitchen window listening, Charity Julius was dragging me to the bedroom and locking me into a closet where I suppose the owner ordinarily kept his guns; it was equipped with a very high outside padlock. At about the moment Angel began to be concerned at not hearing my voice, Charity was calling the ax-man at his job, and he was tearing home in his flashy truck.

I WAS SORE but conscious in the dark closet, which seemed to be full of hard, lumpy things. I hauled myself to my feet, slowly and reluctantly, and waved my hand around above my head. I was rewarded with the feel of the string of the closet light. I gave it a tug, and looked around me in the sudden glare.

There were out-of-season clothes pushed to one side, and the other was occupied with fishing gear. The floor was covered with boots, from lace-up steel-toe leather ones to thigh-high waders.

I hoped Angel would come soon, but something might have happened to her, too. I had better find a weapon of some kind. The fishing poles refused to break into a usable length until I found an old bamboo one. With some effort, I shortened it to about a yard. The thick end was quite heavy, and I thought that if I had room to swing it, I could cause some harm.

"What are you doing in there?" Charity Julius asked from the other side of the door. It seemed prudent not to answer.

"We're going to take care of you, whoever you are," she said raggedly. "No one's found us in all this time, and we'll get the money in four more months. We haven't waited all these years for nothing."

I leaned against the door. "Who's on the roof instead of you?" I asked. I was too curious not to.

"They found them?" It was Charity's turn to be shocked. "Oh, no," she said, so quietly I could barely catch the words.

I wondered why Mrs. Totino hadn't called her granddaughter. She had to know Charity was alive; her live-in lover's presence in the life of Alicia Manigault proved that. So why hadn't Charity known?

I shifted uncomfortably in the cramped space. What was taking Angel so long? A glance at my watch said fifteen minutes had crawled by.

I had a feeling things weren't going my way when I heard the male voice outside.

"Harley! She's in the closet," Charity Julius said, and another piece dropped into place. Harley Dimmoch only wanted his family to call at a certain time because then he, and not Charity, could be sure to answer the phone. He didn't let them come visit without lots of notice because she would have to stay somewhere else.

"Let's see who it is," he was saying, and then I had only the quick rattle of the key in the lock to warn me. I raised the fishing rod and launched myself out of the closet, which almost got me shot dead. The young dark-haired man was holding a no-nonsense revolver in his hands, and at my appearance he fired. Fortunately for me, the fishing rod caught him in the stomach and the shot went high, but at least it settled matters for Angel, who came through the unlocked back door like gangbusters.

The small bedroom was full of shouting, moving bodies, and the fear of the gun.

Charity was so busy trying to grab me that she missed Angel's appearance until Angel justified all her martial-arts training by kicking Charity in the side of the knee, a decisive move, since Charity shrieked and folded instantly, and thereafter lay on the floor moaning.

Harley Dimmoch had grabbed my arm with his free hand and was trying to aim the gun with the other when Charity shrieked. He saw her go down, and I watched his face twist with desperation. He had begun to swing his arm to fire at Angel when she seized it, twisted his wrist clockwise with a curiously delicate grip of her fingers, slid closer to him and under his arm, and then with his arm twisted and extended in what must have been an excruciatingly painful position, kicked one leg out from under him and kept on raising his arm while he was falling until his shoulder dislocated—or perhaps his arm broke.

He screamed and fainted.

The gun was lying on the floor beside his useless arm. With the end of the fishing rod, I poked it into the closet where I'd been imprisoned and shut the door. Angel and I looked at each other and panted and grinned.

"Idiot," she said, "if the gun hadn't gone off, I'd still be out there wondering what was happening.

"Idiot," I said, "if you'd known he'd come home, you could have jumped him out in the driveway and then he wouldn't have had a chance to pull a gun on me."

"What the hell happened to you? I didn't hear a thing after I got around back!"

"She punched me in the stomach and then the neck," I explained, pointing to the young woman clutching her knee on the floor. "That's Charity Julius."

For one second Angel's face reflected the shock I'd felt.

"So the ax-man," she said, "must be Harley Dimmoch?"

"Yep."

Charity tried to get up, gripping one of the cheap pine night tables, but she collapsed back on the floor with a white face and sobs of pain. I was far from wanting to comfort her, and she would have been glad if I'd been in her place, but still, I felt uncomfortable, to say the least.

Angel left the room for a minute and reappeared with some heavy, silvery duct tape and a pair of scissors. She used the tape efficiently on Harley Dimmoch's ankles and Charity Julius's wrists. I held Charity up while Angel worked, shrinking from touching her but having to.

The gunshot had attracted no attention, apparently. No one pulled up, or called, or knocked on the door. We three women gradually calmed down. Charity regained control of herself. Her wide dark eyes stared at us assessingly.

"What now?" she asked.

"We're thinking," Angel answered. I was glad she had. I had no idea what would come next. But obeying an irresistible impulse, I leaned forward and looked into her face and asked, "Who is the third body?"

She closed her eyes for a minute. She must be twenty-one now; she looked older.

"My grandmother," she said.

"Then who is the woman living in Lawrenceton?"

"My great-aunt, Alicia."

"Tell me," I said intently. "Tell me what happened that day." Finally, finally, first among all the people who had wondered, I would be the one who knew. It was almost like being the only one to discover Jack the Ripper's true identity, or getting the opportunity to be a fly on the wall on a hot, hot day in Fall River, Massachusetts, in 1892.

"MY AUNT WAS visiting. She was staying over in Grandmother's apartment with Grandmother."

"How did she get there?"

"She came by bus. My dad picked her up in Atlanta. She had been there three days."

"How come nobody knew?"

"Who was to know? Who was to care? We didn't have many visitors, mostly because Mom was so sick. I didn't talk about it at school. Why would I? And Daddy had been working on the roof for three days, trying to get it finished. Going to pick her up was a pain in the butt, an interruption, but since Mother and Grandmother wanted her to be there, he did it.

"Harley had come to visit me and to help Daddy. I said I was sick and stayed home from school. I don't think they believed me, but they knew how much I missed Harley and they were willing to give me a little slack."

Her face was flinty when she said this. She was willing herself not to feel, as she'd been willing herself not to for all these years.

"Harley—lady, do you think he's okay? He looks awful bad; you should call an ambulance." She had asked Angel, not me.

"He's okay. He's breathing," Angel said with apparent unconcern. But I noticed she was taking his pulse when Charity looked away.

"Harley was up on the roof with Daddy, hammering away. It was the day the patio was going to be poured; they'd spent the morning building the form. Daddy just insisted Harley help him, and Harley didn't really mind, but he had come to see me, and he was going to have to go back home without having talked to me very much. Daddy just didn't seem to understand, it was like when we lived close to Harley and Harley would help Daddy all the time, but then we could go out on a date and be away from them. But up on the roof, Daddy starts this heavy churchy stuff, about how Harley was going to have to stop drinking and learn how to control his temper if he was going to marry me, which was what Harley and I wanted. And he reminded Harley, all this Bible stuff, about keeping his hands off me until we were married, was what it boiled down to.'' She sighed deeply, shifted to try to make herself more comfortable. "Listen, can't you get me a pillow, or something?''

Angel got a pillow from the bed and eased it under Charity's shoulders. Charity was as striking as the newspaper picture had suggested, but even stronger looking, with the large dark eyes and the jawline giving her face character. What kind of character, I was finding out.

"So,'' she resumed, "Harley decides that up on the roof with my dad is a good time and place to tell him we've already slept together.'' She rolled her eyes, the very portrait of an exasperated teenager. Silly old Harley. "My dad went nuts. He was yelling and screaming and swinging his hammer around, and said Harley had to leave and not see me anymore. Harley got scared and mad, and he swung his hammer, and it hit my dad in the head, and he died. Right up there on the roof.''

I closed my eyes.

"Then Harley climbed down and told me. Mama had been over visiting with Grandmama and Alicia in the apartment, and she hadn't heard anything."

Her face twisted with pain, and I felt another pang of guilt. What were we going to do with these people? But she rallied and plowed on, and I could tell she was feeling a certain degree of relief in the telling.

"I knew that Mama would tell. And Harley would go to jail. I'd never see him again. So I told Harley to go back up on the roof, and when Mama came back I told her to go up to the bedroom, lean out the window, Daddy and Harley had something they wanted her to see. So when she leaned out the window, Harley hit her, too." She must have read something in my face, because she said, "Mama was really sick, anyway, she was going to die."

And no traces of the murders had been found in the house, because they had actually taken place on the roof.

"What about your grandmother?" Angel asked.

"Well, I knew she would tell about Mama," Charity said pettishly. "It just seemed to grow and grow. I'd always felt closer to Alicia, anyway. Me and Harley couldn't think of what to do, so I told Great-aunt Alicia what had happened. She and my grandmother had never gotten along good, and sharing that house in Metairie had just made it worse. They had hardly any money, and they didn't have any friends, and she had forged Grandmother's name before, once or twice, and not gotten caught. She said people couldn't tell old women apart anyway. What she told us to do—she thought about the money right away—she said we might as well get it and have a life, rather than going to jail, that Mama and Daddy wouldn't have wanted me to go to jail. So she called Grandmama, and told her Mama was up in her bedroom and was feeling very bad, and Grandmama hurried up those stairs, and when she was in the bedroom looking around, I sort of wrapped my arms around her and stuck her head out the window, and Harley... took care of her.''

My stomach lurched.

I would just as soon not have heard more, but by then I couldn't have stopped her.

''We sat down in the kitchen and talked. Harley was kind of crazy by that time. We couldn't decide what to do with the bodies, or what to tell Mr. Engle, who was coming to pour the concrete in two hours. Then we thought...just leave them where they are. Harley said we should cover them with lime, that's what his dad did when the family dog died and they didn't want other animals coming in the yard to dig at the grave. And up on the roof, we'd get turkey buzzards if we didn't do it... so he went into Atlanta and bought the lime and a gray tarp... he had gotten some blood on his clothes so he borrowed some of my daddy's. Harley got back and fixed them up on the roof, and then he waited.

"Alicia had realized by then that no one knew she was there, so she could pretend to be Grandmama. And she said if I put on Mama's wig, Mr. Engel wouldn't know from a distance it wasn't Mama. And he had to see me as me, too. We'd just tell him Daddy had had to go off on an errand. So Harley drove the truck around behind the garage and hid it while Mr. Engle was there, and I went out and talked to him, and then I ran upstairs and put on Mama's Sunday wig, because she was wearing the other one." For a second the toughness cracked in Charity Julius's face and I could see the horror underneath. "And I went and rattled round in the kitchen so Mr. Engle could see me, and Alicia pretended to be Grandmama."

I had wondered all along why Hope Julius had been wearing her Sunday wig when Parnell had seen her working in her kitchen, yet it had been on the wig stand when Sally had been shown through the house the next day. And I had seen the everyday wig, its synthetic hair fluttering in the breeze on the roof.

"How did you vanish?" I asked.

"It was my great-aunt who realized I had to. We sat down that night and figured it out. Harley had to go home like nothing was wrong. I had washed and dried his clothes by then, and he put them back on and we just put the ones of Daddy's he'd been wearing in a garbage bag...Harley's hairs might be on them or something. And I got in the car with him, not taking hardly anything of mine, just one change of clothes, because Alicia said it had to look like I'd just been taken without notice. I put Mama's wig back on the wig form; my hair was enough like Mama's that I didn't figure it would matter if they found one of my hairs in it. Then Harley, on his way back home, dropped me off at a bus station. I had the key to the house in Metairie. We used all the cash Mama had in her purse to buy the ticket."

"The police checked all the bus stations within a reasonable radius," I said.

"I wore an old pair of Mama's glasses, and I put a pillow in my front like I was pregnant," Charity said rather proudly. "That about knocked Harley over, he really laughed."

For the first time, I met Angel's eyes. She was looking as sick as I felt. I had completely lost my taste for this insider information.

But she went on talking, though Harley was now stirring and moaning. She'd stayed in the Metairie house for a couple of days, eating only what was in the pantry and not going outside. On the third night, she'd slipped out of the house very late, gone to a pay phone at a convenience store a few blocks away, and called her great-aunt, asking her to get a message to Harley. Harley's parents might question a young woman calling at their house. Harley could join her as soon as the investigation died down, maybe in a month, they figured.

"I couldn't stay in the house that long, someone would see me, I knew," Charity said. "I was going crazy."

I was willing to bet that was true; shut in a house, forced to remain invisible, with her last memories of her family closed in that house with her.

"So what did you do?"

"Aunt Alicia cashed one of my grandmother's checks and snuck out and mailed it to General Delivery, Metairie, and after I picked it up, I went to New Orleans and rented a room and found a job. I'd never done any of that before." She sounded rather proud. "I gave them Harley's name and Social Security number. I figured girls could be named Harley, too. And it was a real Social Security number. I had it written in my billfold. I knew everything about Harley."

"And he came down when he figured it was safe?" Angel wanted to cut this true confession short. She (and Harley) were shifting restlessly.

"And got a job at the lumber place. And then we rented this cabin. And here we've been for all this time. Until you found us. Who the hell are you two?"

"I own the Julius house," I said.

"Oh, you're the one Alicia called about. The one Harley was supposed to get rid of. The one who was asking so many questions, with too much time on her hands."

I could have done without Angel's cocked eyebrow.

"But he said he screwed it up. And he was too scared, being back in that area where someone might recognize him, to try again. He was so mad...Listen, I'll bet you don't care, but really I'm in awful pain."

"Why didn't your great-aunt just sell her house and drop the phone number?" It was the last question I really wanted an answer to.

"She and grandmother both had to be there for a house closing; they owned it jointly. And if Alicia cut off the phone, where was she supposed to be? People did call her from time to time...and she had to get her mail somehow. So she got the idea of renting it to that tub of lard, her cousin's daughter, so she could get some money to live on till the estate was probated...four months! We almost made it!"

And her confessional mood changed suddenly to hatred, all directed at me. She actually managed to heave herself at me, despite the broken knee, despite bound hands. I found myself wondering if it were true that Harley had wielded the hammer in all three murders.

"I've had a thought," Angel said, unmoved by Charity's desperation. "If the forensic anthropologist examined those bones the day after you found them, he knew that one skeleton wasn't Charity. He must have told them it was an old woman. So who are the police going to question first?"

"The woman they think is Mrs. Totino."

"Right. So why hasn't she called down here to warn these two? Why didn't she tell them the bodies had been found?"

I could tell from Charity's face she was asking herself the same thing. I was regretting not calling Sally Allison. I would have known so much more. I could have called the police anonymously, if I had figured out Charity Julius was alive; I wouldn't have been so shocked by a confrontation with a woman I thought was dead these past six years. And now we wouldn't be in the strange fix we were in.

"They've got her in custody, or they're watching her so closely she thinks they're tapping her phone calls," I said. "I bet she never called these two from her own phone anyway."

"Think Alicia will break?"

"I bet she will. Not because she's fragile, but because she'll want company, someone to blame the actual murders on. Yeah . . . once they actually question her identity, she can't keep up the pretense that she's Melba Totino, at least not for long."

"This is going to be awfully hard to explain," Angel commented.

That was an understatement.

"I have to go to a hospital," said Harley clearly.

He was badly hurt, and so was Charity, and damned if I knew what to do with them.

"Shelby's not gonna like it if I get arrested for assault," Angel said. I hardly thought Martin would enjoy my arrest either.

"Here's what we're gonna do," Angel told her two white-faced victims. "We're gonna leave, and we'll call the police from a pay phone."

"What fucking good is that going to do us?" Harley asked.

"For one thing, you ungrateful moron, they'll take you to the hospital. Now, I'd like to point out that we could just leave you here to rot, or we could kill you, and I guarantee no one would miss you."

I turned away so the two killers couldn't see the shock on my face.

"We'll tell them you did this," Charity spat. "You'll do jail time."

"No I won't, and I'll tell you why," Angel said calmly. "Because we're not gonna tell the police about Harley trying to kill us. And we're both alive to tell about it, and positively identify him, too. But the minute you tell the cops about us, we tell them about you. At least this way you'll only stand trial on some old charges, with no evidence left to collect or eyewitnesses."

It wasn't much, but it was something, and in the end they agreed. What choice did they have? We wiped my fingerprints off the fishing rod and anything else I might have touched in the closet, and Angel, I saw with some amazement, was wearing plastic gloves. I was feeling uncomfortably like a criminal myself.

They didn't ask why we hadn't told the police about Harley's first attack, thank goodness.

We left the house and didn't speak to each other until after we'd stopped at the next convenience store. Angel was driving again, and she parked rather over to one side so the rental car wasn't readily visible from the clerk's counter. She got out and used the phone. I waited numbly, slumped in my seat.

We negotiated the rest of the drive still in the same silence. When we were once more in our Hyatt room, light-years away from the cabin by the bayou, Angel said she was very hungry, and I realized I was, too. Wastefully, we ordered room service, and while we waited for our food, we took turns in the shower and changing clothes as though we could wash away the morning.

I was depressed and tired and it was just noon. Angel, on the contrary, seemed to have a blaze of triumph about her. For her, I thought, the morning had been a vindication. She had protected my life successfully and proved her worth, her effectiveness. But that triumph was offset by watching the suffering of the nasty couple from whom she'd rescued me; she wasn't cold enough to be indifferent.

When our food came, we were ravenous.

"Think they'll tell?" Angel asked as we swapped bites of our desserts.

"Don't know," I said. "It's a toss-up. Let's go home."

"Good idea. I'll call the airline after I finish this cake."

Within an hour we were on our way to the airport.

SEVENTEEN

WE COULDN'T ESCAPE rain that day. It was pouring in Atlanta. Shelby had maneuvered close to the door somehow, and we loaded in our luggage and got into the car—Martin's Mercedes—with a minimum of fuss. Angel and Shelby were very glad to see each other. Shelby passed a paper over the seat to me; I was buckled in in the back. It was a copy of today's *Lawrenceton Sentinel* and the headline did not pack the punch it would have this time yesterday.

"Autopsy Results Surprising," read the headline, an understatement if I'd ever seen one. In a low voice, Angel began telling Shelby what we had seen and done that morning. I read between the lines of the story Sally Allison had written so carefully. The forensic anthropologist, faced with what seemed a straight-forward job of identification, had been surprised (and perhaps rather pleased) to find his job was more complicated than he'd thought. I would like to have seen Jack Burns's face, and Lynn's, when they found the third body was not Charity Julius. It was apparently Lynn who'd gone to Peachtree Leisure Apartments to find if the purported Mrs. Totino had any ideas about the identity of the third corpse. Ever since the bones had been brought down from the roof, this must have been the moment the old woman had been dreading. Lynn had not allowed Duncan, the security guard, to call ahead, but Alicia must have been watching the closed-circuit TV channel and must have recognized Lynn as the police officer who'd come by before to tell her the bodies had been found. She'd opened the window and jumped.

"How much would they have realized from the murders?" Shelby asked.

"Huh? Oh. The purchase price of the house, the money that Mr. Julius had accumulated to start his own business, and I guess whatever money was due from life insurance policies. I suppose the company has to pay up if the missing person is declared dead. If they just could have gone four more months without the bodies being discovered, the three of them could have scattered to the four winds once the money was in their hands."

"You think she would have given Harley and Charity their share?" Angel asked as we changed highways to go northeast to Lawrenceton.

"I think so. She'd seen Harley in action."

"It must have been galling, to have been so strapped for money all those years—the old woman, I mean."

"Yes, for her. It may not have made much difference to Harley and Charity. They didn't kill the people they killed for money; the money was Alicia Manigault's idea, first and foremost."

A teenage romance that went wrong; the Ballad of Charity and Harley.

I wondered what the Louisiana police were making of the two.

As we entered my hometown, I had a hard time believing I had questioned a seriously injured woman as intensely as I had. I also had a hard time believing she'd hit me in the stomach hard enough to cause the deep bruise even now developing in the soft tissue around my navel.

I hadn't heard from Martin in two days. I wondered how things were going for him in Guatemala. I missed him, abruptly and passionately. Tears began to well up in my eyes, and I took off my glasses to dab at them with a Kleenex.

"Martin called," Shelby said out of the blue. We were turning on the road out of Lawrenceton that led to the house. "He tried your hotel room but found you'd checked out. I have to go back to the airport tonight to pick him up."

"I'll let you, rather than going myself," I told him. I was too tired to face the airport more than once that day, and I would rather be warm and rested and in bed when he came home than tired and wrinkled and public at the airport.

We pulled into the driveway, Shelby trying to tell me about the security systems he'd been investigating while we were gone, me not giving a damn.

"Are you afraid of going in?" Angel asked. The rain was coming down in earnest as we got the bags out of the trunk. We crossed the garage to open the side door and take the covered walkway to the kitchen door. Madeleine sat regally, tail wrapped around her, by her food dish.

"No," I said, and realized it was true, "I'm not afraid of this house. There aren't any ghosts here. The people who would have become ghosts are the ones who are still alive, down in Louisiana. The people who died were too nice to be ghosts."

Now, this babble gives you some idea of my exhaustion, and the look Shelby and Angel gave me simultaneously told me I was becoming weird. But the house didn't scare me; I felt happy to be in it again. I breathed a sigh of relief when the Youngbloods left to go up to their apartment for their own reunion, after I'd refused Shelby's offer to carry my bags up to my bedroom.

The light on the answering machine was blinking. I pressed the "Play" button to hear my messages.

My mother: "We're back, and we had a wonderful time! The message you left saying you were going to New Orleans was kind of confusing, Aurora. Is Martin with you or not? Is this thing about the bodies upsetting you? Call me when you're home."

Emily Kaye: "Roe, I'm sorry to be such a pest, but we really do need help on the Altar Guild. Please call me at home when you get back from wherever you are. Oh, by the way! Aubrey and I are engaged!''

Aubrey: "Roe, if you're upset about the discovery at your house, please call me. I want to help if I can. And I wanted you to know, first—Emily says she'll marry me."

I made a face into the reflective glass of the clock.

My mother: "You know, Aurora, I really wish you had left the name of your hotel with Patty at my office. It's very aggravating not being able to get in touch with you, to make sure you're all right. My understanding from calling Martin's office is that he is not with you. So what are you doing in New Orleans?"

I hoped the antique earrings would soothe her.

The other messages, in order: Sally Allison, Sally Allison, and Sally Allison.

I headed up the stairs, looking at my beautiful house with pleasure, glad to be home. Later my husband would be home; we would talk; everything would be all right.

But when I entered our bedroom I had a sudden picture of a dark-haired girl seizing an elderly lady and forcibly shoving the gray head through the window so it could be stove in with a hammer.

I banished that vision firmly.

This was my house.

PETER TURNBULL

First Time in Paperback

THE KILLING FLOOR

A Glasgow P Division Mystery

REMAINS TO BE SEEN

Social worker Pam McArthur had a talent for making enemies
and wasn't missed much when she disappeared. But when
her mutilated body is found nearly eight months later—head
and hands removed in an attempt to conceal her identity—
Ray Sussock of Glasgow's P Division begins to unravel the
shocking secret that cost the victim her life.

Another murder occurs, this one not so neat, so planned, so
clever, and it puts the squad on the trail of blackmail, scandal
and corruption at the city's very foundation—and a cool,
collected killer who believes he can outwit Scotland's finest.

"Turnbull continues to dazzle..."   —*Publishers Weekly*
Available in October at your favorite retail stores.

WORLDWIDE LIBRARY®

KILLING

HARLEQUIN®

I N T R I G U E ®

The Spencer Brothers—Cole and Drew...
two tough hombres.

Meet

Cole Spencer
Somehow this cowboy found himself playing bodyguard.
But the stunningly lovely, maddeningly independent
Anne Osborne would just as soon string him up as let
him get near her body.

#387 SPENCER'S SHADOW
September 1996

Drew Spencer
He was a P.I. on a mission. When Joanna Caldwell-
Galbraith sought his help in finding her missing
husband—dead or alive—Drew knew this was his
chance. He'd lost Joanna once to that scoundrel...he
wouldn't lose her again.

#396 SPENCER'S BRIDE
November 1996

The Spencer Brothers—they're just what you need to
warm you up on a crisp fall night!

...A DANGEROUS THING
BILL CRIDER
A Carl Burns Mystery

First Time in Paperback

PAINFUL CORRECTNESS

The new dean of Hartley Gorman College arrives with an agenda of political correctness that hits Professor Carl Burns where it hurts: Shakespeare, Milton, Homer, Wordsworth—all of his DWEMs (Dead White European Males) must go.

True, the new curriculum at HGC has wrought some controversy, but when a popular professor takes a fatal flying leap out a window, it's death by anybody's definition.

Between grading papers and vying for the affection of the librarian, Burns discovers a sordid tangle of lust, scandal and secrets that draw him into a chase for an elusive and unlikely killer.

"An amusingly self-effacing...mystery series."
—*New York Times Book Review*

Available in October at your favorite retail stores.

 **WORLDWIDE LIBRARY®**

THING

REBECCA

43 LIGHT STREET

YORK

FACE TO FACE

*Bestselling author Rebecca York returns to "43 Light Street"
for an original story of past secrets, deadly deceptions—and
the most intimate betrayal.*

She woke in a hospital—with amnesia…and with child.
According to her rescuer, whose striking face is the last
image she remembers, she's Justine Hollingsworth. But
nothing about her life seems to fit, except for the baby
inside her and Mike Lancer's arms around her. Consumed
by forbidden passion and racked by nameless fear, she
must discover if she is Justine…or the victim of some mind
game. Her life—and her unborn child's—depends on it….

Don't miss *Face To Face*—Available in October, wherever
Harlequin books are sold.

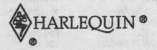

43FTF

CRIMINALS ALWAYS HAVE SOMETHING TO HIDE—BUT THE ENJOYMENT YOU'LL GET OUT OF A WORLDWIDE MYSTERY NOVEL IS NO SECRET....

With Worldwide Mystery on the case, we've taken the mystery out of finding something good to read every month.

Worldwide Mystery is guaranteed to have suspense buffs and chill seekers of all persuasions in eager pursuit of each new exciting title!

Worldwide Mystery novels—crimes worth investigating...

 **WORLDWIDE LIBRARY®**

HARLEQUIN®

INTRIGUE®

THAT'S INTRIGUE—DYNAMIC ROMANCE AT ITS BEST!

Harlequin Intrigue is now bringing you more—more men and mystery, more desire and danger. If you've been looking for thrilling tales of contemporary passion and sensuous love stories with taut, edge-of-the-seat suspense—then you'll *love* Harlequin Intrigue!

Every month, you'll meet four new heroes who are guaranteed to make your spine tingle and your pulse pound. With them you'll enter into the exciting world of Harlequin Intrigue—where your life is on the line and so is your heart!

Harlequin Intrigue—we'll leave you breathless!